No One's Baby

Wanda Taylor

James Lorimer & Company Ltd., Publishers
Toronto

James Lorimer & Company Ltd., Publishers acknowledges funding support from the Ontario Arts Council (OAC), an agency of the Government of Ontario. We acknowledge the support of the Canada Council for the Arts, which last year invested $153 million to bring the arts to Canadians throughout the country. This project has been made possible in part by the Government of Canada and with the support of Ontario Creates.

Cover design: Tyler Cleroux
Cover image: Shutterstock

Library and Archives Canada Cataloguing in Publication

Title: No one's baby / Wanda Lauren Taylor.

Names: Taylor, Wanda Lauren, author.

Series: SideStreets.

Description: Series statement: SideStreets

Identifiers: Canadiana (print) 20190190701 | Canadiana (ebook) 20190190728 | ISBN 9781459414969 (softcover) | ISBN 9781459414976 (EPUB)

Classification: LCC PS8639.A97 N62 2020 | DDC C813/.6—dc23

Published by:
James Lorimer &
Company Ltd., Publishers
117 Peter Street, Suite 304
Toronto, ON, Canada
M5V 0M3
www.lorimer.ca

Distributed in Canada by:
Formac Lorimer Books
5502 Atlantic Street
Halifax, NS, Canada
B3H 1G4

Distributed in the US by:
Lerner Publisher Services
1251 Washington Ave. N.
Minneapolis, MN, USA
55401
www.lernerbooks.com

Printed and bound in Canada.
Manufactured by Marquis in Montmagny, Quebec in December 2019.
Job #181203

This book is dedicated to youth who are struggling with, defending, trying to discover, or have had to deny their mixed identity. You are inherently you, no matter what the rest of the world says.

Chapter 1

Tears and Rain

Warm streams of spring rain pounded down on the empty streets of Joshua Creek. Lizzie Randall watched an orange cat scramble across the dirt road, under a row of perfectly trimmed bushes and between two large, well-kept homes. Lizzie turned back toward the pale-yellow house in front her. She knew Eileen, her adoptive mother, would be waiting for her to walk through the door.

The rain had soaked through Lizzie's thin sundress. She looked down at the flowery blue tights that now stuck to her skinny legs. Rain rolled down her cheeks and fell to the ground. Normally, Lizzie's tawny face was framed by thick, bouncy black curls. But the rain had turned her hair into a slick, dripping mess. She had run all the way there from her boyfriend Damon's house. He had been acting like a jerk again, bossing her around and bursting into fits of anger. Lizzie had been away from home for two whole days. She knew her mom would be upset that she'd missed school. She wasn't sure if her tears were because of Damon or because she knew Eileen and her would likely fight again. She let the tears roll down her face and get lost in the raindrops.

A loud sob overtook Lizzie and she inhaled deeply. Why was she crying? She leaned against the trunk of the old tree at the edge of the driveway. She blinked to clear the water and salty tears from her eyes. Between the sparse cherry blossoms, she saw the glow of a lamp in the window.

As she stumbled toward the front door,

Lizzie could see her mom's shadow moving inside.

When Lizzie entered the living room, her mom let out a loud breath. Eileen was sitting in the dusty brown armchair. Her shoulders were pressed flat against the chair's high back and she was staring angrily out at the rain pounding against the window. Lizzie was confused. Was her mom's sigh one of fury or relief?

Lizzie often wondered why Eileen and her husband, Bill, had adopted her, a black baby. Lizzie had never felt close to Eileen, and they had grown even further apart in the years since Bill died. The waiting up and worrying about Lizzie seemed like the actions of a caring parent. And yet Lizzie never felt that Eileen really cared about her.

Lizzie eased her soaking wet body onto the sofa beside her mom's chair. "I'm sorry, Eileen." The words stuck in her throat. She didn't really mean them.

Eileen didn't respond.

"Did you hear me? I said I'm sorry."

"You called me Eileen," she finally said. Her voice was full of anger. "It's hurtful."

The room went silent.

Finally, Eileen turned to Lizzie. "Oh my God, Lizzie, you're drenched. Go upstairs and take off those wet clothes before you catch a cold."

"I'm fine."

"You're just asking to get sick."

"I said I'm fine."

"Are you?" Eileen scowled. "I can see in your eyes that you've been crying. That crazy Damon sent you on your way again, didn't he?"

"No."

"He did. This is why you must stop sneaking out. You're only seventeen. You still have a lot to learn about relationships. I can't watch you destroy yourself, running with a boy like Damon."

Lizzie squeezed her hands together and bit her tongue. *You mean a black boy like Damon,* she thought. Her eyes searched the lines in her mom's pale face. Their skin, just like their lives, was a world apart. Lizzie stared down at her caramel-coloured fingers, still damp from the rain, then back again at Eileen. All she saw as she looked at her mother were reminders of their differences.

Damon made Lizzie sad when he got angry, but she knew that was because of the passion they felt for each other. But her mom's anger just felt cold and made her feel unwanted.

"You used to do as you were told, Lizzie," Eileen went on. "I just don't know what to do with you when you do these things."

"What things?"

"Sneaking out, missing school, coming in at all hours."

"I'm not a child anymore."

Eileen got up and pulled her cardigan closed. She headed out of the living room.

"You hate me because I'm not really yours!" Lizzie blurted out.

Eileen turned, her eyes wide. "Hate you, Lizzie? I don't hate you. I love you. That's why I'm mad as hell. You never call. You stroll in and out whenever you want to. You keep sneaking off to be with that troublemaker. I want more for you than this. You should be applying to universities. Instead you're skipping school. You should be planning for your future. Instead, you're putting your life in the hands of a boy who cares about himself more than about you. Damon doesn't love you, but you can't see it. I have a horrible fear that you'll leave with him one day and never come back."

Lizzie couldn't look at her mom. *I don't believe her*, she thought. Eileen was just trying to control her. And trying to keep her away from the boy she loved.

Eileen turned away and left the room, leaving Lizzie in the glow of the crystal lamp, fighting back her tears and anger. Lizzie picked up a sofa pillow and punched it over and over until her arm got tired.

Soon, Lizzie's eyes began to get heavy. She felt exhausted. She tossed the pillow to the floor and wiped her face with the back of her hand. The room went dark as she turned the knob on the crystal lamp. Lizzie felt her way up the stairs to her room. Still wearing her wet clothes, she climbed under the sheets. She closed her eyes and prayed for sleep to come quickly.

Chapter 2

Best Life

Damon: Im sorry . . .

Lizzie read Damon's text and rolled back
over. She'd lost count of how many of his
sorrys were stored on her phone. The text from
Damon reminded her of the argument they'd
had, and the one she'd had with her mother.
Lizzie loved Damon, but was the first to
admit that he was carrying a lot of rage. When
Damon was ten, his parents had split in a nasty
divorce. Right away, his mother had brought

home a new boyfriend, a white man who treated both Damon and his mother badly. It made Damon angry because he couldn't defend himself or his mother. Now, when he lashed out in anger, Lizzie was the nearest target.

Damon: babe are you up?

"Now I am," she mumbled to herself. Lizzie put the phone on silent and slid off the bed. She was still wearing her clothes from the night before. The hem of her sundress was curled up and had dried into a wrinkled mess. She grabbed a pair of leggings and a T-shirt from the closet. She pulled a pair of panties and a bra from her top drawer and went to take a shower. When she got back, her phone was flashing. There were at least a dozen messages from Damon.

Damon: k call me when u wake up then

Damon: i love u

Damon: come on . . . text me back

Damon: let's talk Im calling ur fone

Damon: Lizzie stop ignoring me!

Lizzie turned up the sound on her phone. Right away, another text came in.

Damon: I'm coming over there!

Lizzie: I was in the shower chill out

Damon: all morning??

Lizzie: What do you want Damon

Damon: wanna see you. Can i come over?

Lizzie: U know my mother doesn't want you here

Damon: that's cuz she dont want u with a black guy

Lizzie sighed. Even if she felt like Damon might be right about that, she could never tell him. Eileen often argued that she never denied Lizzie's colour, that she only wanted the best life for her. She would tell Lizzie that the realities of race would come against her in the real world. She said that she was critical of society, not Lizzie. All that had done was confuse Lizzie. She felt what she really needed was understanding and support from her mom, not lessons in reality. She needed to feel free to talk about the pain of not knowing her biological mother or vent about her relationship with Damon. In Lizzie's mind, none of that had anything to do with race, and everything to do with being a mother.

Lizzie sent one last text to Damon: I'm coming over

Eileen was washing dishes when Lizzie got to the kitchen. There was silence between them as Lizzie poured milk and cereal into a bowl. She could tell her mom was fighting to hold back words. Lizzie sat at the table, waiting for whatever lecture was sure to come.

Eileen placed the last dish into the strainer, wiped her wet hands on her shirt, and sat down across from Lizzie. "You're going to be late for school, Lizzie. Finish up with that bowl so I can wash it."

Lizzie shoved her bowl across the table toward Eileen. The thought of eating breakfast made her stomach turn over. "Here, I'm done."

She got up from the table.

"Lizzie."

Lizzie grabbed her phone and headed toward the front door.

Eileen followed. "Lizzie, I didn't mean for you to get up without eating your breakfast."

"Yes, you did. You just can't help yourself."

"Not true."

"You wanted my bowl. I gave it to you. I'm leaving."

"I'll get your bookbag for you."

"I won't need it."

"Lizzie, I didn't want us to start another morning off like this."

"Us? You started it. You always start it."

"I was angry last night. I know I should have stayed downstairs and talked to you. But you have to understand, you deserve so much more than Damon."

Lizzie was tired of hearing how much she deserved when still didn't know what that meant.

"Damon's not good for you," Eileen continued. "He's going to lead you down the wrong path."

"Are you finished?" Lizzie asked coldly. "I don't want this lecture right now."

"It's not a lecture. I'm trying to get through to you, Lizzie."

"By trashing my boyfriend? I'm tired of you talking bad about him all the time. You won't even take the time to get to know him."

"I've asked around. He's not a stable guy, Lizzie. I'm just afraid that his anger will turn into violence. Violence against you."

Lizzie wouldn't admit that she worried about the same thing herself. She needed to hold on to her certainty that it was about race. "Sounds like you've asked everyone except me. Well, I'm glad your uppity white friends were able to fill you in on my black boyfriend, the thug."

"What is getting into you, Lizzie? Listen to the words coming out of your mouth."

"Are we done?"

"We're going to finish this conversation when you get home from school."

"Not going to school. I'm going to Damon's."

Lizzie stomped through the door and slammed it behind her. She decided to walk to Damon's instead of waiting for the bus, which only ran on the hour. She needed the walking time to burn off her frustration. She knew that Damon had problems with his anger and that he was a high-school dropout. But she had to defend him against Eileen's judgment. To Lizzie, the criticisms of Damon felt like an attack against her too. As she walked, she wondered if it would have even been an issue if her birth mother had been the one to raise her.

Would her real mother have been more understanding? Would she have given Damon a chance? Lizzie wondered if Eileen could ever understand a black daughter the way a black mother would.

Half an hour later, she turned up the path to Damon's house. *After my defending him, he'd better do a lot of apologizing for yesterday*, she thought.

Chapter 3

Surprising News

Lizzie sat in the waiting room of the Joshua Creek Clinic. She kept wringing her hands. She couldn't control the twitching of her leg back and forth.

After Damon had apologized for their fight and cooked her a special dinner, Lizzie had forgiven him. Like she had done many times before. But Lizzie's fights with him and her mom had upset her and tired her out more than usual. She hadn't been feeling right for a couple of weeks. But it wasn't until she missed her period that her friend Priya convinced her she should see a doctor.

The nurse approached her with a smile.

"Lizzie, come on, dear. You're next."

Lizzie followed the nurse into one of the small offices. She sat on the chair across from the doctor's seat and rested her elbow on the desk. She read the posters on the walls and tried not to think about what the doctor would say when she walked in.

DO YOU NEED HELP DECIDING?

The words spread across a poster taped to the closed door. Lizzie looked away.

The doctor came in and plopped into the black swivel chair. She pushed her glasses up her nose and swept locks of wavy blonde hair from her face. She had way more energy than Lizzie expected. Was that wide smile a sign of good news or bad news? Or was she just trying to hide her pity for the skinny black teenager sitting in front of her?

"Hi, Lizzie. I'm Dr. Adams. How are you feeling?"

"Okay," Lizzie lied.

"Well, I'm not sure if this will be good news or bad news for you. Your test came back positive. You are pregnant."

Lizzie was silent.

"Do you know what you plan to do?" Dr. Adams asked. "I can arrange for one of the counsellors to speak with you."

"No, thanks. I'll be fine," Lizzie lied again.

"Do you have any support? I mean from the baby's father or your parents?"

"Yes." Another lie.

"Okay, then, that's great. A lot of the young girls who come in here don't have anyone to turn to. Or they haven't told their families that there was even a possibility that they were pregnant. Many of their parents don't even know they're sexually active. So, I'm glad your parents will be supporting you."

Lizzie wasn't sure if she could get up and

leave. She could barely hear a word the doctor was saying. She wanted to disappear into the burning sinkhole that used to be her stomach.

The doctor was still going on. "If you decide to keep the baby, you should come back for another appointment. Or see your regular doctor if you have one. Also, get started on some prenatal pills as soon as possible. You will need those vitamins to make sure you have a healthy, happy baby. If you decide you will keep it, that is."

"Okay." Lizzie still had no idea what was being said. She looked for a sign on the doctor's face that she was finished. There was none.

"Is there anything you want to know, Lizzie?" The doctor's smile was still there.

Lizzie decided it was pity. The doctor felt sorry for this newly pregnant stranger. Lizzie wondered if the doctor could sense her fear. What was she going to do?

"You must have some questions. I know this can be very confusing."

"No." One last lie. She had a million questions, and she was more than confused. But she couldn't bring herself to ask the doctor anything or tell her how afraid she was.

"Okay. But please come back if you need to, Lizzie. And I encourage you to get the prenatal vitamins. The folic acid helps in the baby's brain development . . ." Her words faded as Lizzie thought about what Damon would say. What her mother would say. What her friends at school would think of her.

Lizzie finally saw the signal in Dr. Adams's face. "Thanks again," she muttered. She got up and dashed out of the doctor's office.

Lizzie caught the bus straight to Damon's house. He was the first person to tell. Damon would guide her and tell her what they should do.

The bus ride to Damon's house was long and painful. Lizzie practised in her head how she would break the news to him. She imagined his possible reactions. Like scooping her up and swinging her around the room with excitement. Or talking about getting a place together and being a family. She felt too young for all that, but if Damon thought it could work, she was willing to give it a try.

A smile came across her face as the news from Dr. Adams began to sink in. In just a few months she would be somebody's mother. The thought was horrifying and exciting and scary all at the same time. And she knew her birth mother must have felt exactly the same way when she found out she was pregnant with Lizzie.

Chapter 4

No Future

Damon was playing Call of Duty when Lizzie let herself in without knocking. He didn't hear her at first. She slipped off her shoes and rushed over to the sofa.

Damon jumped. "You're here!" He smiled and put down the controller on the coffee table.

"I didn't mean to scare you. The front door was open."

"It's okay, I'm just happy to see you." He kissed both of her cheeks, then her lips.

"Is your mom here?"

"No, she's at work."

Good, Lizzie thought. It was going to be hard enough to tell Damon the news. She wasn't ready to include any parents in that conversation. She hadn't even thought of when and how to tell her own mom yet.

"Why you looking for my mom all of a sudden? You're all kinds of shy when she's here."

"I just wanted us to talk in private."

"Damn, Lizzie, how many more times do I have to say I'm sorry? I cooked for you and everything."

"Not that." Lizzie's heart was beating fast.

"I don't like it when we fight. Sometimes I just don't know what gets into me."

"Damon . . ."

"Hey, I got a surprise for you!"

Damon leaped from the couch and ran upstairs. Lizzie felt like she would vomit. She just couldn't get the words to leave her mouth.

Damon returned with a tiny box. "Open it." He jammed the silver box into Lizzie's clenched fingers.

She stared at it. Was he proposing to her? She was nowhere near ready to be married. Was it a bracelet like the one he'd broken during one of their fights? It had been her favourite: a gold heart-shaped pendant with her initials engraved in it that dangled from a tiny gold chain. Or maybe it was a necklace. After all, he had stolen her only necklace and sold it at the pawnshop when he was desperate for money. He had promised to buy it back but never did.

"Open it," Damon urged again. Sensing Lizzie's hesitation, he asked, "Babe, what's wrong?"

Lizzie burst into tears. She couldn't hold back her feelings any longer. Becoming a parent was both frightening and foreign to her. In that moment, she realized her whole world and everybody in it was about to change.

Damon shifted closer to Lizzie on the sofa and cradled her in his arms. He rocked her and crooned, "It's okay, Lizzie, I'm here. I know something is bothering you. Tell me what's the matter."

The words came rolling right off Lizzie's tongue. It was like her words left her mind and took over all the space in the room. She sobbed, her face buried in Damon's chest. "Damon, I'm pregnant. I just found out today. And I've been walking around like a zombie trying to figure out how we could have been so careless. And how we're going to raise a child. And how we are going to tell our parents about it."

Lizzie cried until she noticed Damon had stopped rocking her back and forth. His grip around her shoulders tightened. She waited for him to say something, but he was silent. She looked up into his eyes. "Damon . . ." she said.

He pulled his arms away and left her side. She watched him as he stood in front of the living-room window, staring out at the sky and shaking his head defiantly. "No. No. No. No." He kept repeating it over and over.

"Damon!"

He turned toward her. His eyes were like black dots and his eyebrows were pushed together so he looked like a menacing bulldog. "This can't happen," he blurted out. "You can't keep it. You can't."

"Damon, can we talk about this?"

"No! There's nothing to talk about. You're getting rid of it! I had no plans in my life to be a father. Not after what I went through with mine. You will never force me to be anyone's dad."

"Why are you being like this?" Lizzie was scared and confused. "Damon, I don't know if I have the guts to have an abortion. That's killing." The words coming out of her mouth surprised her. She wasn't sure when she'd started thinking that way about abortion. Maybe it was when she realized her birth mother had faced the same decision she was facing now. But her excitement turned to fear again. Her heart sank when she realized Damon didn't want to become a family with her.

Damon marched over and snatched the silver box from Lizzie's hand. "Get out!" he screamed. "You tricked me, Lizzie. You are trying to trap me into being with you. How could you be so lowdown and sneaky? I can't even look at you. Get out. And can you just, please . . ." Damon looked pained, like he hated the words coming out of his mouth. ". . . just lose my number. We're done."

Lizzie was shocked. She never imagined Damon would react so badly. She thought he would calm her fears and tell her they would be okay. That they would get through it together. That they could start planning their future together.

Lizzie looked down at her feet to make sure they were still planted on the ground. It confirmed for her that what just happened was real. She stood up on weak legs that felt like overcooked noodles, then crept to the door.

She took longer than usual putting on her shoes, hoping Damon could feel her heart breaking. Hoping he would change his mind and wrap his arms back around her. Instead, he stood there with his hands on his hips. He didn't say another word. She feared he would never speak to her again. Without saying anything, Lizzie slipped out the door and never looked back.

Chapter 5

Looking for the Past

Lizzie waited until Eileen's blue Volvo pulled all the way down the driveway and rounded the corner before replying to her friend Priya's text.

Lizzie: She's gone. Come.

Lizzie and Priya had been friends since Priya's family moved to Joshua Creek from Bangladesh. Lizzie and Priya had grown up on the same street. They were both shy and felt they didn't fit in. Priya's culture and the way she belonged in it drew Lizzie in ways she didn't really understand.

Lizzie ran downstairs to greet Priya. The girls hugged, then Lizzie pulled Priya into the house, slamming the door behind them.

"What is this news I must miss my chemistry class for, Lizzie?" Priya mimicked her mother's lilting speech pattern.

"Come in the kitchen and sit down."

Priya followed Lizzie and sat at the table, facing her. Then she said in her usual voice, "Girl, the suspense is killing me. Spill."

"Okay. I'll just come right out with it. Priya, I'm pregnant."

"Get . . . out . . . of . . . here!" Priya's mouth fell open once the words were out.

"I just found out a few days ago."

"And you waited this long to tell me? Does Damon know?"

"He wants nothing to do with the baby, or me."

"That creep. Sorry."

"It's okay. He is a creep."

"Does Eileen know?"

Lizzie shook her head. "I haven't been able to tell her."

"Lizzie, you have to tell her. She's your mom."

"I know, I know. I need to tell her, but it never seems like the right time to bring it up. And she will be so mad at me."

"What are you going to do?"

"I'm going to have the baby."

Priya slapped her hand over her mouth. "So, you're going to be a mother?" she asked around her hand, then dropped it. "Lizzie, are you ready for that?"

"Of course not. But it's happening anyway."

"Eileen will have you committed." Priya laughed.

Lizzie couldn't find a chuckle to return. "She has no room to judge me."

"I wasn't trying to upset you," said Priya.

"I'm just saying. Do you think she wants a little brown grandchild running around this racist neighbourhood? You know how much she cares about what her friends think. You and your mom barely get along. How is she going to feel about this baby?"

"I've been thinking about that a lot, Priya," said Lizzie. "Why does she get a say about my baby? It was her job to have a say about me, about my background. But I don't think she ever stuck up for me. I heard her trying to justify her choice to adopt me by saying things like 'she's different in a good way' or 'we wanted to make a difference.' What does that shit even mean?"

"You make her sound like she took you in as a charity case."

"Maybe she did. Dad didn't see me that way. Did you know he showed me some papers about my birth one time? I was only about twelve, but I remember it."

"Papers? So, you know who your birth parents are?"

"No. Dad said I could have my actual adoption records unsealed once I turned eighteen."

"Yeah, but I've heard it's not so easy. Some parents don't want to be found."

"Dad said the papers had my birth mother's last name. It was Collins. And they went to Kingston to get me. I was born at Kingston General Hospital."

"Lizzie, we need to write a movie about this. You know that, right?"

"But you get why it's so important for me to keep this baby, right? Just think. If my birth mom had made the decision to get rid of her baby, I wouldn't be here talking to you right now. I legit owe my life to her, for giving me my first home for nine months. I owe at least that much to this baby."

"Whoa, that's way deep, Lizzie. I guess I never thought of it like that."

"I never had either. But this baby has me thinking a whole lot of crazy thoughts."

"Those thoughts are not crazy. If you can't talk to Eileen, do you want to talk to my mom about all of this?"

"What? Hell, no!"

"I mean because she's a therapist." Priya laughed.

"I know. Yeah, I'll pass."

Priya got up and picked up her backpack. "I really want to stay here and chat with you all day. But I'm not a school skipper like you are."

They giggled as Lizzie walked Priya to the door.

"Lizzie, you know I've got your back," said Priya, suddenly serious. "I will support you through this. But you've got to tell Eileen, okay? She deserves to know."

The girls hugged out their goodbye. Lizzie watched as Priya strolled down the driveway toward school. All day, thoughts played on repeat in Lizzie's mind. A new baby. A black baby in a neighbourhood that could cause a child to feel uncomfortable in their own skin. The rejection

Lizzie thought for sure would come from Eileen. No calls or sorry texts from Damon in days. A mother who had carried Lizzie long enough to give her life, only to abandon her. If her biological mother had even half the thoughts and feelings Lizzie was having already, how could she possibly have decided what to do? There was a hole in Lizzie's life she knew could only be filled with answers to questions like that. How could she bring a child into the world when she knew almost nothing about herself?

Lizzie abandoned the idea of going to school. There were just too many thoughts taking up the space in her head. She climbed into the shower and tried to drown her thoughts under the pounding of the hot water.

When her mom got home from work, Lizzie was flipping aimlessly through the TV channels. It was well after six. "I stopped to grab us some subs on the way home," Eileen said. "I didn't feel like cooking, and I knew you wouldn't have made dinner."

"Nope."

"Come to the kitchen and eat. I don't want to have to clean up a mess in the living room. And I don't want to eat alone."

Lizzie turned off the TV and followed her mother to the kitchen. The smell of cold cuts mixed with pickles and onions made her stomach turn. Lizzie sat down and opened her sub, pretending to want it. By the time she removed the wrapper, Eileen was already biting into her sandwich and chewing eagerly. Lizzie did all she could to keep from running to the bathroom.

"Eat up, Lizzie," said Eileen. "I got yours with extra pickles, the way you like it."

Lizzie took a bite and forced it down.

"How was school?"

Lizzie could not pretend any longer. The smell, the taste, the sight of the onions. She pushed her plate away. "Mom . . ." Lizzie choked out the words. "I don't want the sub, thank you. But I do have something to tell you."

"I'm listening."

"I have a lot of questions about my birth mother. And it's not to hurt you. I just need to know who I am."

"You know who you are. A beautiful, strong young woman. A young woman with a bright future and a world of potential. Nothing you find out about your birth mother will change that. Where is this coming from?"

"You know, I think about this often."

"Has this really been bothering you? Is that why you've been skipping classes? Why didn't you just talk to me?"

Lizzie didn't realize until then that she had already made up her mind. "I'm leaving Joshua Creek, Mom. I'm going to find my birth mother. I know you don't approve, but —"

"Damn right I don't approve, Lizzie. You don't need to do this now. And certainly not on your own."

"I want to. And I'm going. I'm not asking your permission. I'm just telling you what's up.

This is something that's important to me. I just want you to understand and be okay with it."

Eileen tossed her half-eaten sub back on the plate. She wiped her mouth with a napkin and stormed upstairs. The look on her face shook Lizzie. She would have preferred that Eileen argue with her. At least then she would have some idea where she really stood with her adoptive mother as she ventured out on her own to find her birth mother.

Tears dripped onto the plates as Lizzie cleaned up. She wondered if she was doing the right thing by not telling Eileen about the baby. Had she totally destroyed their fragile relationship by choosing the blood parent over the adoptive one? Lizzie went back to the sofa and sat alone with her tears.

Chapter 6

Alone

"Lizzie, I'm just so surprised by this," said Priya. "I mean, I know you need to do this. But I never thought you would make it official so soon. You only found out you were pregnant a couple of weeks ago!" Priya's voice was loud in the quiet ice cream shop. She slapped a finger to her lips when she realized the couple in the booth next to them had turned to look.

"I know, I know," said Lizzie. "But the more I sit around thinking, the more I feel like it's something I have to do. And with things so bad between me and Mom, I keep feeling like there is another mother out there I need to connect with. I know it sounds crazy."

"I wish I was brave like you."

Lizzie scooped up another spoonful of ice cream. "I asked my mom for those papers last night."

"You did?"

"I tapped on her bedroom door and asked if I could have them. She didn't answer me."

"That sucks. So how will you even find this woman?"

"I'll look up last names in Kingston. I'll research people who are around the same age as her."

"But, Lizzie, Collins isn't exactly a rare name. You have nothing to go on."

"I thought you were on my side."

"I am . . . but . . . so, you're just going to walk around Kingston asking strangers with your mother's last name if they know of a woman who gave her baby away seventeen years ago? I mean . . ." Priya threw her hands in the air and shook her head.

"Google is a gift, Priya. I know the city. Maybe I'll find a relative, someone who knows something."

"I don't know, Lizzie."

"I have to do this, Priya."

"I know. But if Eileen knew you were pregnant, she would never let you go to Kingston alone."

"She wouldn't be able to stop me." Lizzie stood up. "I should get going, I have to pack my stuff."

"You have a place to stay in Kingston?"

"I found an Airbnb. I used Mom's credit card to book it for a week."

"She's gonna see that on her credit card statement!"

"Yeah, like next month."

"I can't believe you're going. Are you scared?"

"Yes."

"Do you want me to drive you to the bus station? I can get Mom's car."

"Okay."

"And after I drop you off, text me every minute, okay? I'll be worried about you."

"I will."

×××

When Lizzie got home, she bypassed the kitchen, knowing that was where Eileen would be. It was Saturday, Eileen's laundry day. Lizzie could hear the popping of the washer and the dull hum of the dryer. She decided to wait until she was packed and leaving before confronting her mom.

Lizzie's phone buzzed as she pulled a red duffle bag from her closet. She tossed the bag on the bed with a pile of clothes and picked up the phone.

Priya: just bumped into Scotty, can I tell him ur leaving?

Scotty had had a crush on Lizzie for a long time. He wasn't her type, but she was flattered by his attention.

Lizzie: what's he doing there, he doesn't even eat dairy, lol

Priya: I'm not at Dave's, left right after you did. He's standing in my face asking about you, what do I say

Lizzie: tell him about the birth mother, not about the baby

Lizzie tossed the phone aside after Priya sent a brown thumbs-up emoji. She chose her clothes deliberately. She wanted to take comfortable clothes. But she thought she also should have some nicer things on hand in case she was able to track down her mother and arrange a meeting. Eileen's tap on the door startled her.

"Come in." Lizzie started rolling clothes and stuffing them into her bag.

Eileen appeared in the doorway. She folded her arms.

"So, you're really doing this?"

"Yup."

"I need you to know I am totally against you being hundreds of miles away in Kingston."

"I know. I know you don't approve. But I still wish you would support me."

"Lizzie, I can't support this. Kingston is a city of transients. What if your mother spent time in one of the jails there? What if she was living some dark, violent existence?"

"This is about you thinking my real mother will replace you."

"No, it's about you being too young. It's about the outside world not being as forgiving as the world you've grown up in."

"Is this a lecture about my skin being brown?"

Eileen unfolded her arms and moved to sit on the bed. She motioned for Lizzie to sit beside her.

"Do you know why I'm always after you about school and your future?"

"Because you're mean?"

"Seriously? Lizzie, my job is to look out for you. As a biracial girl, you can be great — you are great. But people will only see the outside. Your father and I wanted to give you the best life we could. And I want that to lead to a nice career and a comfortable life for you."

"I don't care what other people think of me. You seem to care too much about it. Or maybe you're just embarrassed by me."

"That's not true."

Lizzie thought about the times she'd heard her parents argue about race — her race. It seemed to her that colour was more of a concern inside her home than outside. She always thought her lack of closeness with kids at school was because she wanted to be different and not part of the crowd. She never thought it was because they might not want to be around her because she was brown.

"Why are you talking about this right now?" Lizzie asked, even though she no longer wanted to listen. She got up from the bed and continued rolling clothes and stuffing them into her bag.

Eileen stood up and watched Lizzie pack for a moment. Then she reached into the pocket of her jeans and pulled out a roll of twenties, which she tossed on the bed.

Lizzie pretended not to see it.

"Lizzie, take the money. You'll need it," Eileen said, her voice softer. "I can't stand the thought of you ending up on the street with no options, like some kind of runaway." Eileen sighed and left the room.

Chapter 7

The House with the Blue Door

The Joshua Creek Bus Station was packed when Lizzie and Priya pulled up. As soon as the bus arrived, passengers rushed to be first to board. Priya squeezed Lizzie tight.

"If you hug me any longer, I'm gonna cry," Lizzie said.

"Sorry," Priya said. "Don't forget to text me every minute."

"Okay."

Lizzie got on the bus and moved toward

the back. She wanted to slip into one of the few empty seats and disappear. As soon as she sat down, an Asian woman slid in next to her and pulled out a romance novel. *Good, I won't have to talk*, Lizzie thought. She put her headphones in and turned on Cardi B full blast.

xxx

The bus jerked into the Kingston Terminal, shaking Lizzie awake. She peered out the window. It was dark. Kingston looked flat and lonely. She sighed and checked the time on her phone: 9:47. Since she had been sitting at the back of the bus, Lizzie was one of the last to get off. She stood for what felt like a lifetime waiting for the passengers ahead of her to gather their bags and make their way off the bus. As she waited, she searched through her cellphone contacts and found the taxi number she'd saved the night before.

"Can I have a taxi to the Kingston Terminal, please?" she said in a loud whisper.

"Name?"

"For Lizzie."

The driver must have been just around the corner. His white Ford Fusion was already near the bus idling when Lizzie stepped off. He had a flashing light on top of his car, bigger than the tiny orange ones she was used to seeing in Joshua Creek. Within a few minutes the driver was pulling up to the Airbnb address.

"Eight dollars, Miss." The driver smiled.

Lizzie handed him exact change and said goodbye. The Airbnb was a two-storey brick house. She tapped lightly on the front door. No one came. She waited for a bit, then knocked again. A worn piece of tape covered the doorbell. Lizzie pushed it, just in case it worked. Finally, a woman with curly grey hair peeked through the door.

"Hi," said Lizzie. "I booked an Airbnb at this address."

"Are you Lizzie?"

"Yes."

The woman opened the door wider. "Goodness, young lady, your check-in time was three o'clock. It's almost ten."

"Sorry, I missed my first bus and the second one was delayed."

"No, I'm sorry. You should have messaged me. When you didn't show up, I took another booking for that room. A couple and their baby came around five. I refunded your money back through the Airbnb. Didn't you go online and check?"

"I wasn't really sure how it all worked. I never used Airbnb before."

"My page clearly states my rules. Sorry, dear, the space is gone. If you're stuck, Chelsea Place is not far from here."

She closed the door gently, leaving Lizzie standing alone in the dark.

"You're kidding me!" Lizzie screamed to no one. She plopped down on the front step and typed Chelsea Place into her phone's map. The Chelsea Shelter for Girls popped up. It was a twelve-minute walk away. Lizzie hoisted her heavy duffle bag across her shoulder and started off.

The walk to the shelter felt more like twelve hours than twelve minutes. Lizzie was exhausted by the time she reached the driveway. There was a tilted wooden sign that read Chelsea Shelter for Girls. Lizzie gazed down the winding driveway to see an old house with a wide porch and bright blue front door. She groaned as she made her way toward it. Her hair was now frazzled and messy. She patted it down, hoping that would make her look more presentable. She knocked, and a woman soon came to the door.

"I'm looking for a bed for the night," Lizzie said between tired breaths.

"Come on in."

Lizzie stepped inside and dropped her duffle bag to the floor.

"Bring it in here. I'm Daniella, one of the staff here."

Daniella motioned for Lizzie to follow her back to a small office. Lizzie watched as Daniella squeezed her heavy thighs behind the cramped desk and sat down. Lizzie sat in the wooden chair on the other side of the desk.

"You're lucky. I have one empty bed left. We had someone who didn't come back tonight. Now, we only take up to age twenty-three, so if you're not twenty-four yet, you can stay here. We also don't take anyone under seventeen. But we won't put you out on the street. If you're sixteen or under, we can call Children's Services. They will help you out."

"I'm seventeen," Lizzie said. She had no idea what Children's Services was, and she didn't want to find out. She wondered why a kid who was younger than sixteen would be wandering around alone looking for a place to stay. The thought made her sad.

"Okay, can you fill out this form?" Daniella shoved a clipboard toward her. "It's very basic. Name, contact information, social worker's name if you have one."

Social worker? Lizzie thought. *What am I doing here?*

Lizzie was almost finished with the intake form when she came to a question about whether she had any children.

"Need some help?" Daniella asked, noticing the worried look on Lizzie's face.

"Just this question about children."

"Oh, just skip that one. You're not a mom, are you?" Daniella smiled.

Besides Damon and Priya, Lizzie had not told anyone about her pregnancy. She'd never spoken the words out loud to anyone but them.

"I'm pregnant."

Chapter 8

Taken In

At Lizzie's words, Daniella's face and body shifted and her eyes widened. She slapped her hand on her forehead and sat straight up in the chair.

"Pregnant. Pregnant?" she repeated.

Lizzie wondered if she had made a mistake telling her. Had she ruined her chances of a free bed for the night?

"We don't take in pregnant girls here, Lizzie. For one thing, we don't have the space nor the facilities to house an infant," Daniella said.

"But I'm just here for the night."

"So you're not homeless?"

"No. Yes. I mean . . ."

"The young women in this shelter are homeless, Lizzie. They have no place else to go. But if you have a family and a home . . ."

"I'm not a runaway."

"Are you sure?"

"I had a place booked but I lost it. I'm not from here. I plan to find another place in the morning."

"I only wish it was as easy as you're making it sound, Lizzie. Why are you in Kingston? This city is not like a lot of others. With the prisons, the university, and the military college, a lot of people come and go. Are you a student? Or relocating to be closer to a family member who's in prison?" Daniella folded her hands on the desk, waiting to hear Lizzie's story.

When Lizzie thought about the university students making Kingston their temporary home, she felt some guilt for all the classes she'd been missing. "I'm trying to find my mother. I mean, my birth mother," Lizzie said.

"And you think she's in prison?"

"No . . . I mean . . . I don't know. I was adopted into a white family. They were good to me. But now that I'm pregnant, I feel like I need to find out who me and my baby really belong to."

"Okay, I don't need to hear more. You are very young, Lizzie. It seems to me you should be doing this with your parents' support. The ones who raised you. But I guess that's not for me to judge. I really wish you all the best with this search, but I've seen a lot of young women on their own in this city. And too many times the only journey they made was a quick spiral downward."

Lizzie was crushed. She felt her hope leaving the room.

"Tell you what," Daniella said. "I will give you this bed tonight. You can stay here until you find something else. But only if you don't tell any of the residents you're pregnant. I don't need to set any precedents or start any wars around here. We've got enough problems."

"Thank you so much." Lizzie was relieved. She marked no beside the parent question and handed the form back to Daniella.

"Follow me. Are you hungry?"

"Starved." Lizzie hadn't eaten since she'd left Joshua Creek.

Daniella made Lizzie a snack and watched as she wolfed it down. Then she led Lizzie to a tiny square bedroom at the top of the stairs. Inside were two single beds and two dressers. An old lamp sat on each dresser.

A heavy-set, dark-skinned girl was lying on one of the beds reading a magazine. She looked up as Lizzie and Daniella entered.

"Lizzie, you'll share this room with Stella for the night," said Daniella. "She's been around for a while, haven't you, Stella?"

"Hi," said Lizzie shyly. "I'm Lizzie."

"So?" Stella growled.

"Stella, please be nice," said Daniella. She turned to Lizzie. "I'm going to let you settle in. Just pop downstairs if you need anything. We serve a light breakfast at eight in the morning."

Daniella left the room and closed the door. Lizzie went to the bed at the far side of the room. She rummaged through her bag to find a shirt and shorts to wear to bed. She could feel Stella staring at her, but tried to ignore it.

"Girl, you must be desperate," Stella finally said.

Lizzie ignored her. She was afraid to say anything that might make her new roommate mad.

"You got a deaf problem too?" Stella demanded.

"I don't want any trouble," Lizzie answered. She wondered if Stella was the reason the other girl didn't come back.

"I don't like sharing my space." Stella tossed her magazine to the side and sat up.

Lizzie started to feel nervous. "I'm only

here until the morning. I just needed a place to sleep."

"Aren't you half? Where's your white mama? Probably out screwing another brother, right?" Stella got up, making a point of banging into Lizzie on her way out the door.

Lizzie wanted to cry, but fought back the tears. She quickly changed and climbed into bed. She turned toward the wall and tried to fall asleep.

Lizzie's heart stopped when Stella burst back into the room. Stella came straight to Lizzie's bed and stood over her in silence. Lizzie could sense the girl standing there, but was afraid to move or turn around.

"Sleep with one eye open, pretty light-skinned girl." Stella laughed and got into her own bed.

Why does Stella want to hurt someone she doesn't know? Lizzie wondered. Was it because Lizzie's skin was lighter? What kind of life did Stella have that she would hate another black girl because of the shade of her skin?

Lizzie tried to breathe lightly in the silent room. She stared at the wall until she finally heard Stella's breath deepen and the other girl began to snore. Finally, Lizzie was able to relax. Daniella's offer that she could stay for as long as she wanted was what Lizzie needed. But the thought of sharing another waking moment with Stella was absolutely frightening. As much as she desperately needed to, Lizzie knew she couldn't stay here.

Chapter 9

Shade

The next morning, Lizzie woke to the sound of voices downstairs. She looked around the room and was glad to see that Stella was gone. Her bed was made. Lizzie wanted to clean up, eat, and get out of there. She was glad Stella had left her alone all night, and she didn't want to do anything to set her off.

After a quick shower, Lizzie went downstairs to the dining room. Seven other girls were sitting around a long table eating breakfast, including Stella.

"There you are, Lizzie," Daniella chimed. "Come, sit down and join us. There's space beside Stella."

Lizzie looked over and saw Stella roll her eyes. Since there wasn't anywhere else for her, Lizzie walked over and sat in the chair. The girls passed bowls of food to her so she could fill her plate.

The woman sitting to Lizzie's right poured juice into a glass for her. "I'm Abbie," she said. "I'm on staff here."

"Why don't the rest of you introduce yourselves to Lizzie?" Abbie said. She smiled. "Make her feel welcome."

"Even if she's not?" Stella barked.

"Stella . . ." Daniella warned.

"I'm Gina," a scrawny blonde girl chirped.

The rest of the names came from around the table.

"I'm Dawn."

"I'm Chantel."

"Rebecca. But everyone calls me Becky."

The girl's bashful grin showed missing and rotted front teeth.

"I'm Clover. Hi."

"Juana," the last girl said. Her chubby face was friendly.

Lizzie smiled. This was a better start than she'd had with Stella. "Hi, everyone," she said.

Stella looked annoyed. Lizzie hungrily scooped food into her mouth, but she kept an eye on Stella's hands and quick movements.

"So, this may be my last few nights here," Becky sang. "My social worker said he can get me a bed in rehab — finally."

"That's good news," Abbie said, smiling. "You've been waiting on this for a long time."

Clover clicked her teeth and sighed. "Hope that works out for you." She went on, speaking so fast that Lizzie could barely understand her. "I went through that shit so many times. Was in rehab twice. Third time, I signed myself out 'cos they were a bunch of asshole flakes. Went to detox about a dozen times. In and out. In and out. Couldn't deal with it. Those crackers don't do nothing for you, really. I think half of them are on drugs themselves. Anyway, none of it ever worked for me. I wouldn't be getting so excited about going to any treatment around here if I were you."

"Maybe she doesn't have all of your crazy-ass problems, Clover," Abby said. "Her dad didn't kick her out at thirteen."

As Lizzie ate, she noticed there was a lot of chatter and gossip floating around the table. The girls seemed to be okay with sharing their life struggles. It made Lizzie feel like an outcast. Some of the stories of family troubles and crime shocked her. What they were saying was different from anything she ever went through, or had even heard about.

Lizzie began to feel bad for the way she'd left things with Eileen. She decided she would take the time to call her mom later. But her priority was getting herself out of the shelter and someplace safer, away from Stella.

Lizzie finished her breakfast. She wanted to

slip away from the table to collect her things. Some of the girls were finished eating, but they stayed at the table chatting. Two of them had carried their dishes into the kitchen, and Lizzie thought she should do the same. As Lizzie got close to the kitchen door, she could hear the two girls whispering about her.

"What do you think of the newbie?" one of them said.

"You know black girls," replied the other. "Don't let her innocent face fool you. She's a hood rat just like the rest of them. Can't be trusted."

Lizzie walked into the kitchen and dropped her dishes in the sink. Her appearance didn't stop the girls from chatting. And their giggling was more than Lizzie could bear. She knew it was directed toward her. She washed her dishes quickly and headed upstairs.

Up in her room, she could still hear the girls in the dining room talking about their struggles. She began to see how their lives had led them to the shelter.

Lizzie wanted to believe she was like the other girls. She was facing difficult problems at a young age, wasn't she? But Lizzie knew she was kidding herself. What she was going through was hard for her, but it was mostly her feelings she had to deal with. She had never been abused or abandoned. She had never lacked for food or clothing or a place to live. She had never had to find her own way on the streets. She had never turned to drugs or sex to escape her situation.

Lizzie felt like she needed to leave home, but she realized she had options. This made her even more determined to find her birth mother. She needed to finish what she had set out to do. And the last thing she wanted was to hear Eileen tell her how foolish she was for thinking she could do it on her own.

Once Lizzie had gathered her things into her duffle bag, she tossed it on the floor. As she began to make the bed, Stella appeared in the doorway.

"Taking off in a hurry, aren't you?"

"Yeah, well, I only planned to stay for the night."

"Must be nice to come and go whenever you want. You think you're better than the rest of us here, half-breed?"

"Of course not."

"Why'd you come here?"

"I told you, I needed a place to stay for the night."

"To get to where? Girls who end up here don't have any place else to go. You can't just waltz in and out, sticking your nose in the air. I knew you're nothing more than an uppity light-skinned bitch."

There, she'd said it again. Lizzie knew some black people resented lighter-skinned people. But the prejudice dated back to the history of slavery in the United States and Canada. How could resentment from generations ago have any effect on her life? Finding herself in this strange bedroom with Stella standing over her, Lizzie felt like she was going to find out.

Chapter 10

Fight

"Look, Stella," Lizzie said as calmly as she could. "I don't know you and you don't know me. But really, I try to get along with everybody. I haven't judged you in any way. I don't even care about colour, or shades of black." She didn't dare tell Stella that her adoptive parents were white.

"A person knows when they're being judged. I saw how you were turning up your nose at us girls downstairs."

"That's not what I was doing. I just felt bad for everyone's situation."

"Because you're better than us, right?"

"No."

"I'm tired of uppity girls like you looking down on us. I've had enough of it!"

Without warning, Stella hauled back and landed a punch to Lizzie's face. It stunned Lizzie and she stumbled back. But she quickly composed herself and took a swing at Stella. She missed. Stella grabbed Lizzie by her hair and flung her across the room, slamming Lizzie against the wall. Two pictures fell to the floor from the force of her body hitting the wall. Lizzie jumped up and reached out to grab Stella. But Stella leaped out of the way and Lizzie fell against the dresser. Stella rushed up as Lizzie tried to stand, and dropkicked her back to the floor. Lizzie tried to up again but was met with another punch to the face. She banged against the dresser again, then fell onto her back. By now, her face was cut and bleeding. Stella straddled Lizzie's waist and hit her several more times in the face.

"What the hell is going on in here!" Daniella came rushing into the room. Abbie and several of the girls were behind her. Some of the girls gasped when they saw Lizzie's face.

"Oh my God! Stella, what have you done?"

Daniella and Abbie pulled Stella off Lizzie. A couple of the girls helped Lizzie to her feet.

Lizzie's mouth was full of blood.

"Bitch, are you crazy?" Juana screamed at Stella. "You could have killed her."

Lizzie felt ashamed. She grabbed her duffle bag off the floor and pushed past everyone who was blocking the doorway. She ran down the stairs and out the front door, ignoring the voices calling her name and yelling for her to come back.

When Lizzie glanced behind her, she saw Daniella standing in the doorway calling her name. Lizzie turned and ran down the winding driveway. She refused to look back again. She never wanted to see that blue door and the people on the other side of it again.

At the end of the street, Lizzie stopped and sat on a wooden bench. She cried as she wiped the blood from her face. Juana soon appeared and sat beside her.

"I'm so sorry about what happened to you," Juana said. "Stella is a monster."

"I never did anything to her," sobbed Lizzie. "Why is she so mean?"

"Last year, her stepfather killed her mother. He almost killed Stella. Then he got found not guilty. Stella has been mad at the world ever since."

"Shit."

"He was a white guy. Always going on about how dark and ugly Stella was. So she probably came for you because you're half. She says the lighter the skin, the more people can get away with murder."

"Why doesn't she get some counselling?"

"I think she just needs to find her way. She has nothing and no one. But she didn't have to do this. What are you going to do now?"

"I don't know. I have to find another place to stay."

"Put this in your phone." Juana waited for Lizzie to pull out her phone. "Carla Baker. She's a social worker," Juana said as she added the number to Lizzie's contacts. "She works with youth, and she's really good. She got me the place at Chelsea and is helping me go back to school. I don't know what your deal is. But whatever it is, Carla can help. There's not too many like her out there, so you need to get in touch with her right away."

Lizzie thanked Juana and watched as she made her way back to the Chelsea Shelter for Girls. Blood mixed with tears covered Lizzie's face as she made her way toward where she remembered seeing a Tim Hortons the night before. She wiped her face with the back of her hand. But the more she wiped, the more blood seeped out of her cuts. And she couldn't stop crying. The path in front of her became blurry from the tears, but she kept walking. A few drivers slowed down and stared at her with puzzled looks. But no one stopped to ask if she was okay. She was relieved when she finally saw the big red Tim Hortons sign.

It was crowded inside the coffee shop. Lizzie dashed straight to the washroom before anyone noticed her face.

She shrieked when she looked at herself in the mirror. She almost didn't recognize herself in the swollen and bleeding face. *No wonder people were staring*, she thought. She splashed her face with cold water to try to clean off the blood and stop the tears. She pulled a stack of paper towels from the dispenser and dried her face. She was still sniffling as she keyed in the number for the social worker.

"Hey, are you almost finished?" a loud voice yelled from the other side of the door. A series of vicious bangs followed when Lizzie didn't answer. Lizzie put a hand over one ear so she could hear the voice on the other end of the phone. The banging kept on as the social worker gave Lizzie directions to her office.

When Lizzie was finished the call, she opened the door. There was an older woman standing there with her hands on her hips. She looked homeless. Several bags full of clothing and other items hung from both shoulders.

"You think you own this bathroom?" the woman growled. Most of her teeth were missing. Her hair was dirty and tangled, like it hadn't been washed in years. The strong, sour odour coming off her caused Lizzie to gag. She covered her mouth and nose as she quickly passed by the woman.

When she got outside, Lizzie felt queasy. She wasn't sure if it was because of the smell of the woman or the beating she'd received. She could feel the inside of her mouth watering and she knew she had to vomit. When she could no longer hold it, Lizzie dropped her bag and ran to the filthy black garbage can near the side of the building. Her whole body hurt each time she threw up.

Chapter 11

Help

At the sight of Lizzie being sick into the garbage can, a man coming out of Tim Hortons stopped. Lizzie ignored him and wiped her mouth.

"I'm not going to leave you here unless I know you're fine," he said. His voice was gentle, but firm.

"I must have eaten something bad," Lizzie said. "I'll be okay."

"Do you live around here? I can give you a ride home."

"I don't live around here." She picked up her bag.

"Where are you headed?"

"None of your business."

The man's smooth brown face looked kind and his eyes didn't seem to hold any threat. But Lizzie wasn't ready to trust a stranger.

"Why do you even care? You don't know me!" she barked.

"You're a young girl. You look like you're in trouble. I just wanted to see if I could help out, that's all."

"I don't need any help."

"I think you do. Looks like someone did a number on your face."

Lizzie began marching out of the parking lot.

"Can I at least buy you a coffee and donut?" he called after her.

Lizzie couldn't figure out why he wouldn't just let it go. "No thanks. I don't drink coffee," she yelled back.

He ran up to her. "Look, I know I'm

a stranger. But kids around here know me because I work with at-risk youth. My name is Curtis Jackson, and I'm a social worker." He flashed the ID tag dangling from his neck.

As Lizzie looked at the picture on the tag, Curtis went on. "I'm out here on the streets five days a week helping kids like you. I don't have any dark motives. It's just that I couldn't walk away knowing I could have done something to help you out. How about I buy you a warm peppermint tea to calm your stomach?" His smile was warm.

Lizzie nodded her head and followed Curtis back into Tim Hortons.

xxx

The tea felt good going down. It seemed to settle Lizzie's now-empty stomach a bit.

"So, do you want to tell me where you're from?" asked Curtis. "Honestly, I don't mind giving you a ride home, or to a hospital to get your face looked at."

"I'm not going to a hospital," said Lizzie. "And I'm not going home. I just left there."

"Oh?"

"Here's the story. I'm adopted. I was raised by a white family and I'm trying to find my birth mother."

"And she's here in Kingston?"

"I think so. I'm not sure."

"Where are you staying?"

"I don't know. I got in a fight with a girl at Chelsea and left. One of the girls there hooked me up with some worker named Carla. I'm on my way to go see her."

"Carla Baker?"

"I think so."

"She's one of my coworkers. Yeah, Carla is great. Our offices are just around the corner."

Lizzie began to feel relieved. She had never had anything to do with social workers before. But they played a part in almost all the stories she had heard that morning at Chelsea. Some of the girls clearly resented them for interfering. But it seemed to Lizzie that social workers gave families the kind of support she always thought parents were responsible for.

By the time her last drop of tea was gone, Lizzie had told Curtis most of her story. She put the empty cup down on the table.

Curtis sat there waiting. "So?" he said.

"What?"

"Shall we walk over to the office?"

"I thought you had a car. Didn't you offer me a ride earlier?"

"I did. But my car is parked at work. I was hoping to get you to walk and talk with me so I could figure what happened to you."

"Guess I won't be needing that ride then." Lizzie smiled. "You already know my story."

As they walked the short distance to the office, Curtis talked about his job helping homeless teens. Lizzie felt so comfortable with him, she lost her nervousness about meeting Carla.

When they got there, Curtis led her to Carla's office and introduced them.

"Hey, Lizzie," Curtis said as he left. "Drop by and say goodbye before you leave. My office is just at the end of the hall."

"Okay."

"Come, sit down, Lizzie," Carla said. She led her to a small area with a sofa and chair. There were lots of plants, and beautiful artwork on the wall.

Carla was shorter than Lizzie had thought she would be — not even as tall as Lizzie. She wore her hair in a style Lizzie thought looked like a mushroom, and her forehead was hidden under straight blonde bangs.

"You sounded so upset when we spoke on the phone," Carla said. "Do you want to talk about what's happening? Then I can decide how I can best help you."

After a long conversation, Lizzie felt she was on a good path. Carla said she had found Lizzie a place to stay. One of her clients had just moved out of the space. It was at a home for pregnant girls, where there was a small apartment available for each girl. Carla explained that the home included offices, meeting rooms, and a classroom where the girls could upgrade courses. One of the requirements of living there was that Lizzie would have to attend parenting classes with the other girls. For a warm, free place to stay, Lizzie had no problem following that rule. She thought being around other girls who were also pregnant for the first time could be a good way to find support and friends. And she didn't plan to return to Joshua Creek until she'd found her mother.

Lizzie walked over and peeked into Curtis's office after she left Carla.

"All set up?" he asked.

"Yes, Carla is amazing. She found me a place to stay."

"That's great. Carla has a lot of solid connections in Kingston. Lizzie, I've been curious about your family, ever since you spoke to me earlier. I'd like to help you with that if I can."

Lizzie's face lit up. "That would be awesome," she said.

"Would you like to come for dinner sometime and meet my wife, Gail? She works at Kingston General, and she may be able to narrow down the search a bit."

"I would love that," said Lizzie.

"As a black man, I know it's important to feel attached to your culture and your heritage. Not feeling like you belong to a community must be really hard."

As Curtis handed Lizzie his business card, he added, "I still think you should get that face looked at."

"I will," she lied.

Lizzie left the building feeling relieved. She had a place to stay and someone she could trust to help her find her mother. *Things can only get better from here*, she thought.

Chapter 12

Fitting In

The first few weeks Lizzie was living at the home for pregnant girls was different than she thought it would be. She wasn't able to spend much time searching for her mother because she was too busy just trying to survive. She spent her first week and a half in Kingston recuperating from the cuts and bruises from the fight with Stella. Then she had to search secondhand stores for used furniture for her apartment. Once she was set up, she ran into some other roadblocks. Lizzie had never lived alone. She had never had to worry about buying groceries and cooking for herself. The social assistance money that Carla helped her apply for never seemed to be enough. On a few occasions she called Carla crying. Carla came to her rescue with a food voucher or toiletries. Lizzie wondered how other girls without jobs got by without running out of money for food.

Lizzie was texting Priya every day or so, but she still couldn't bring herself to call Eileen. She wanted to have some promising news first. Otherwise, she thought Eileen would give her a lecture. She would tell her she didn't know what she was doing and pressure her to come back to Joshua Creek. Lizzie wasn't ready to have that conversation yet. She wanted Eileen to see she could make it on her own. She realized she wanted Eileen to be proud of her.

Lizzie had been living at the complex for a month when a few of the girls surprised her with a visit. Lizzie grinned as she opened her apartment door to three girls holding out a chocolate cake. One candle burned on top.

"Girl, let us in!" Deena hollered. "This flame is gonna blow out in a minute."

Deena was the first girl Lizzie had met when she moved in. Her tall frame and brick-red hair made her stand out among the other girls. She was white, and Lizzie often thought Deena would have fit in better than Lizzie in Joshua Creek. But Deena came off as sharp, like she could handle anything.

Lizzie moved aside to let the girls into her room. Cassie and Beatrice had arrived at the home just after Lizzie. Lizzie's bad experience with Stella at Chelsea had kept her from rocking the boat here. She had followed Deena and her take-charge attitude from the start. Cassie was a spunky Indigenous teenager who didn't let anyone tell her what to do. Lizzie was more cautious. Cassie didn't agree with everything Deena said or did, and she made that clear when she needed to. Deena didn't like Cassie's defiance. Beatrice was a shy, blonde seventeen-year-old who didn't want any trouble. She had ended up at the shelter because her parents lost their home and were living in a tent city downtown. She didn't share much with them about her baby or her boyfriend. Lizzie was fine with that. She didn't share more than she needed to either.

"Cassie made the cake, so eat it at your own risk." Deena grinned.

The other two girls laughed, and so did Lizzie. It felt good to be accepted.

"Don't clown my baking," Cassie warned. "Unless you can do better."

"I'll be the first to admit I can't cook a can of beans!" Beatrice smiled.

"You can cook, can't you, Lizzie? Black girls can throw down when it comes to cooking." Deena's hand was on her hip.

"Ooh, yeah, I love me some soul food." Cassie rubbed her stomach.

"I'm a horrible cook," Lizzie admitted.

"That's crazy. You ain't black then." Deena clicked her teeth.

Lizzie wasn't sure how to defend herself against the comment.

"Your mom didn't teach you how to make soul food, Lizzie?" Cassie asked.

"No. She didn't have time." Lizzie swallowed hard as she spit out the lies. Eileen never even thought about looking into ethnic cooking for her. Lizzie believed Eileen wanted her to accept the world she was given, not the one she was born into. So, Lizzie had no experiences she could share related to her black heritage. And that made her uncomfortable.

"Well, you need to get Felicia in apartment seven to show you how. Don't be telling people you're a black girl who can't cook soul food! They'll laugh at you," Deena wailed.

Lizzie was glad when the talk finally shifted to babies. After cake and a lot of talk about nausea and swollen ankles, Beatrice and Cassie said it was time for them to head back to their apartments. Lizzie thanked the girls for bringing the cake and for being thoughtful friends. They hugged her and disappeared. Lizzie sat on the couch next to Deena.

"I noticed you've picked up some pretty neat things to make your place look good," Deena said.

"Yeah, Carla's been helping me with that," Lizzie said, picking up the paper plates and plastic forks.

"Government money? Don't take those damn handouts, Lizzie. You know, you pay for that in never being able to have a life or do what you want. Those social workers own you. But nobody owns Deena."

"I don't have a job . . ."

"Neither do I. But I get what I need. I don't need their blood money."

"You steal?" Lizzie asked.

"Hell, no. If you're interested, I can introduce you to a friend of mine."

"What kind of work is it?"

"Let me know if you're serious and I'll bring Jeremy over. He can explain everything to you."

"Sounds shady." Lizzie didn't want to offend Deena, but she had learned that being raised by Eileen and Bill had kept her sheltered from a lot.

"Hey, I don't tell just anybody my business. Do you want money? Or do you wanna be a dumb puppet for a few measly government dollars?"

Lizzie thought about the life of privilege she'd left behind in Joshua Creek. She had always taken for granted there would be enough money to cover anything she wanted. Now it was a daily challenge, counting money and stretching it as far as she could just to get by. She never had to scrape for money before, and she wasn't very good at making it work.

"Okay, I'm in," Lizzie announced.

xxx

The next evening, Deena showed up at Lizzie's apartment with Jeremy. He was tall and black. His dreadlocks were pulled into a ponytail that hung down the middle of his back. She could see he worked out, as the tattoos on his muscles popped beneath the arms of his T-shirt. Lizzie felt like his big dark eyes pierced through to her soul. She was almost embarrassed by how good-looking he was. When he smiled and said hello, her cheeks felt hot.

"Come in," Lizzie sighed.

Jeremy sat on the chair in the corner. Deena and Lizzie sat together on the sofa.

"See, Jeremy?" Deena grinned. "I told you she was cute."

"She is." Jeremy sat staring at Lizzie, a smile on his face. At first, Lizzie was flattered, but when his gaze wouldn't move from her, she began to feel uncomfortable.

Lizzie decided to get right to the point. "Deena said you have a way for me to make money?" Her voice cracked with nervousness.

"I do," replied Jeremy. "But not just anyone can make this kind of money. I need to know I can trust you to be discreet. You need to keep my business on the downlow."

"What do I have to do?"

"Look, you have a face and body that can make us a lot of money. But it's a risky business. You have to do exactly as I say. In return, I'll make sure you're completely safe and your pockets stay full of cash."

"I don't know what that means."

Jeremy and Deena looked at each other and laughed.

"Ahh. This is a special one, Deena. She's a special one." Jeremy waved a finger in the air. He stood up and looked out the window. It reminded Lizzie of how Damon had stood and thought before he flipped out about the pregnancy.

"She's a little green, sure," Deena said, pleading her case. "But you've seen green before, Baby."

Lizzie was a little confused when she heard

Deena refer to Jeremy as "Baby." Were they together? Was he the father of Deena's baby?

Deena turned to Lizzie. "Trust me, Lizzie. I would never put you in a bad situation. Jeremy knows what he's doing. You just need to trust him."

"I don't even know him."

"But you know me. Trust me."

Lizzie felt like she didn't have a choice. She wanted to make money and loosen the government's grip on her life. "Okay," she said finally.

"Good." Deena clapped. "Go put on something a bit more presentable. Then we'll go over to my place."

Jeremy and Deena waited while Lizzie went to her bedroom to change. She kept trying to guess what the two of them were up to. As a follower, she had come to trust Deena. If Deena said she wouldn't put Lizzie in harm's way, Lizzie believed her. And Deena always had a lot of nice stuff. *How horrible can this job be if*

Deena's doing it? she wondered.

When they got to Deena's place, Deena showed Lizzie to her bedroom. It looked like something from a magazine. There were lace curtains and a queen-sized bed. Everything in the room was red and black, shiny and silky. The rose petals scattered around the floor were soft as velvet.

"What are we doing in here?" Lizzie asked.

"Jeremy has some friends who pay top dollar for favours."

"What favours?" asked Lizzie. She started feeling like she had got into something she didn't like.

"Just sit on the bed beside me and follow my lead. When it's over, you'll go back home with more money for one hour than your paycheque for a nine-to-five."

Lizzie climbed on the bed and waited with Deena. Within minutes, an older man with a beard entered the dimly lit room. His fat belly popped through his suit and hung over his belt.

"Come on in," Deena said in a slinky voice.

By the time Lizzie realized what was going on, Deena was already removing her clothes and Lizzie's. The man watched with an eager grin. Deena sensed Lizzie's reluctance and shot her a silencing look.

Lizzie allowed Deena to continue while the man stared. Then Deena started caressing Lizzie's body. Lizzie felt awkward and embarrassed. She wanted it to stop, but she didn't know how Deena and the man — and Jeremy — would respond if she changed her mind.

After several minutes, the man climbed on the bed with Lizzie and Deena. Lizzie watched in disgust as Deena and the man had sex right in front of her. It was clear this was not the first time Deena had done it with the man. After they were finished, he rolled over, gasping for air.

"C'mon." Deena motioned for Lizzie to follow her out of the room. Lizzie grabbed her clothes and started putting them on. Deena walked out of the room naked. Jeremy was drinking liquor at the kitchen table. "Went good?" he asked.

"As good as it could for a newbie, Baby." Deena smiled.

Jeremy reached in his pocket and pulled out a wad of one hundred-dollar bills. He handed two of them to Lizzie.

"This is your cut. See you next time." He put the wad back in his pocket and returned to his drink.

Lizzie stood there staring at the money in her hand.

Deena pointed to the door. "We'll chat tomorrow, Lizzie," she said.

Lizzie ran back to her apartment. She threw the money on the table and backed away from it. The bills felt dirty. Lizzie felt dirty. She jumped in the shower and tried to wash away the feeling. The memories of the evening and the thoughts she couldn't get to leave her mind. She had no idea what she would say to Deena the next time they saw each other.

Chapter 13

Straight Talk

Lizzie's hand shook as she folded the money she'd left on the table the night before. She realized she was in over her head. She stuffed the money in her top drawer and went to see Cassie. She was mortified by her experience with Deena and needed someone to talk to. She wasn't sure how she would bring it up, but it was eating away at her. Was she now a lesbian? She tapped lightly on Cassie's door.

"It's open!" Cassie yelled. She squealed

when she saw it was Lizzie. "Hey, Lizzie. Come on in. I'm just making some lemonade. You want some?"

"Yeah, thanks."

Lizzie sat at the table. Cassie poured two glasses.

"What are you up to today? I think I felt my baby kick this morning." Cassie gulped down half her lemonade.

"That's amazing." Lizzie sipped her lemonade and tried to figure out how to tell Cassie about what had happened with Deena. "Cassie, how much do you know about Deena?" Lizzie finally asked.

"Not much. Why?"

"Do you know anything about her work?"

"Ha! Sure."

Lizzie was shocked. "You know what she does?"

"Sure. Don't you?"

"No! Well, I didn't."

"She's a ho. Everyone knows that."

"Nobody told me that."

"Why would anyone need to tell you? What do her choices have to do with you?"

Lizzie didn't answer.

Cassie frowned. "You got something you want to tell me, Lizzie?"

Lizzie felt her cheeks heat up. She couldn't get the words out.

"Come on now, Lizzie," said Cassie. "Don't tell me that skank tricked you into her shit?"

Lizzie nodded her head in shame.

"Oh God, Lizzie."

"I had no idea what she was bringing me into," said Lizzie. "I want to throw up just thinking about it."

"Are you okay?"

"Trying to be."

"You have a baby to think about. You can't get yourself caught up in Deena and Jeremy's mess."

"She has a baby to think about, too."

Cassie burst into laughter. "I like Deena,

but I don't think she's really invested in her baby. She's more worried about recruiting girls to make money for Jeremy so he won't leave her."

"So, they are together?"

"Yeah, in her mind. I think Jeremy is just using her. I don't even think he's the father. But he'll only let her keep the baby if she finds other girls to take her place once she gets too big. They need to get new blood in there to keep those dirty old men paying."

"Oh my God!" wailed Lizzie. "I feel so stupid."

"Don't feel stupid, Lizzie. They tried that shit with me, but I already knew their game. I can smell bullshit a mile away."

"I'd never even heard of this kind of thing before."

"Oh, it happens a lot. And in Kingston, there's a lot of criminal stuff because we have so many prisons here. You know, people getting out and committing more crimes. Students doing a bunch of crap on the weekends. The students at the military college can be even worse than the Queens University bunch."

"I really had no idea," said Lizzie. "How do you know so much?"

"My parents and I moved to Kingston to be closer to my brother Val," explained Cassie. "But they spent so much money on his legal defence that we lost our house. He got sentenced to life. And now that we're homeless, I guess we got a life sentence, too. Some white guy accused him of stealing his car from the gas station. He had an alibi, but the gas station cameras were not working. Because he's a young guy from the reserve, they decided he was part of an Aboriginal gang and convicted him of robbery for the benefit of organized crime. They'd already decided he was guilty."

"Cassie, that's horrible."

Cassie shrugged, but Lizzie could see the anger underneath. "My point is, I know the streets. I've lived on them. I know scammers. And white girls can get away with that stuff around here. Everyone turns their head and pretends they don't see anything. Especially the staff in this place. But let you or me do something like that and we'll be out on our asses. Being black or Indigenous around here can be like a death sentence. We're either drunk Indians or black ghetto thugs. I'm surprised you don't already know this shit. Where did you live, under a rock?"

"Joshua Creek. So yeah, I guess it was like living under a rock. Cassie, I need to tell you about me. I was raised by white parents."

"Huh?"

"I'm adopted. I don't even know who my real parents are, let alone the black side of me."

"So, you let me rag on about white people and you're one of them?"

"I'm still black."

"Did you experience any racist shit, or did they keep you away from all that?"

Lizzie thought about the comments she'd heard her mother make in the past. *Our Lizzie is different in a good way* and *we wanted to make a difference.* She always thought Eileen was trying to prove to her friends that she was a good person for taking in Lizzie. But now something else occurred to Lizzie. Were her parents trying to give her a life free from judgment? Was that what Eileen meant by making a difference? Lizzie had never thought about her words in that way.

"I did experience some incidents," Lizzie admitted. "But mostly just staring. Or my parents' rich white friends judging them for adopting a black kid. But all this stuff you're saying about white girls getting away with stuff, I guess I saw that."

"Some shit, huh?"

"Yeah."

"So, what did Deena make you do? Did you go all the way with some dirty old dude?"

"No! But I watched her do it."

"Gross. That's disgusting."

"I can't get the pictures out of my head,"

Lizzie said, mocking horror, then joined Cassie as she laughed. "I'm happy I came to talk to you, Cassie. I feel so stupid. I don't know how I fell for Deena's line. And Jeremy . . ."

"He's one fine specimen, isn't he?"

"Gosh, he's gorgeous."

"Yeah, what a waste."

"He gave me two hundred dollars."

"Bullshit!"

"Seriously."

"Let's go shopping, girl! That's a payday!" Cassie joked. "If my mother hadn't given me these damn morals, I'd go work for them myself."

They laughed together again. Lizzie sipped the lemonade, feeling better than she had since she walked into Deena's place the night before.

"The stuff I'm going through here is so different from my life in Joshua Creek," Lizzie mused.

"Parents can't shelter their kids forever," Cassie said. "Eventually you grow up and learn how twisted and messed up the world is. Even if you didn't come here, you would have found that out sometime. I'm only two years older than you, but I feel like I've lived two lifetimes longer. You have to be careful. Stop being so naïve. Stop falling for everyone's bullshit. That's straight talk."

"I appreciate the straight talk, Cassie."

"Anytime. Now that will cost you two hundred dollars!" She grinned.

Lizzie hugged Cassie and left. But back in her room, she couldn't get Cassie's story out of her mind. She felt bad for Cassie's situation. To know racism could actually manifest itself in such an ugly way shocked her. She wanted to know more about the system that discriminated against Cassie's brother and landed him behind bars for life.

Hearing about Cassie's parents losing their home made Lizzie realize how much she was missing hers. For the first time, she wondered if she was acting like an ungrateful daughter by not appreciating what her parents had given her. Bill always told her she shouldn't let what people thought stop her. The support Bill always gave her when he was alive was the very support she missed now. But she also wondered if Eileen might have been supporting her in a different way. With her constant eye on what people thought, Eileen's view of how people would judge Lizzie was closer to the world Lizzie was now finding herself in. Lizzie thought about all the girls she had met since coming to Kingston. Their lives had been tough and unfair. Maybe Eileen wanted better than that for Lizzie. Lizzie wanted to believe that was the truth.

Chapter 14

Not Black and White

Lizzie let out a sigh as she entered Curtis's office number into her cellphone. She had started to reach out to him twice before but got scared. Curtis and his wife might find a connection at the hospital, might find someone who could lead Lizzie to her birth mother. The thought terrified her, even though it was what she wanted more than anything. At first she thought it was a good thing. But the more it seemed like it could become a reality, the more she became afraid of what they might find.

Once she had learned she was adopted, Lizzie had made up a story for herself. She pictured her mother as a young brown woman with perfectly sculpted hips and a tiny waist. She had soft gingerbread-coloured skin, but her afro told the world she was an activist. Not a woman to be messed with. Lizzie imagined her father as an educated white man. A scholar with his head buried in books, under pressure from his parents to go to law school and take over their family law practice. When they discovered he had got a young black girl pregnant, they'd sent him away, far from his love. The heartbroken girl left behind couldn't bring herself to raise a baby all by herself and gave her up for adoption.

Lizzie was startled when Curtis answered the phone on the first ring. It shook her out of her daydream of what she wanted her parents to have been.

"Good morning. Curtis Walker here," came the voice over the phone.

"Uh, hi," Lizzie responded shyly.

"Hello?"

"Umm, Curtis, it's Lizzie."

"Oh, hey, Lizzie. Never thought I'd hear from you again. You never called."

"I've been trying to settle in."

"Of course, of course. Well, I'm glad you called. How are things going in your new place?"

"It's a learning experience."

"For sure. That's called growing up fast." He chuckled.

"I'd like to take you up on that offer of help."

"About your birth family? Yeah, sure, I can talk to my wife. If she's on board, we'll have you over for a chat."

"Okay."

"Call me back at eleven. I'll call Gail now."

"Thanks, Curtis."

"Don't thank me yet. We have no idea if anyone at the hospital can help. Or what could be waiting for us on the other side of this mystery."

After she hung up with Curtis, Lizzie played scenarios over in her mind. What if her father was not a rich lawyer and her mother a heartbroken schoolgirl? What if they were like Cassie's family — broken, homeless, and fighting a system that discriminated against them? What if her mother was in prison, thinking every day about the bad choices she'd made in her life? What if one of those bad choices was getting pregnant with Lizzie? What if neither of them wanted anything to do with her, ever?

Curtis's words echoed in Lizzie's head, and her mind fought against what her heart had been telling her to do. She started to have second thoughts about going forward. She felt like she would die if her mother refused to meet her.

When she called Curtis back, he sensed the change in her voice. He convinced her just talking to his wife wouldn't force Lizzie into any kind of decision. He offered to pick her up. Instead, she decided to make the twenty-minute walk to his office. That would give her some time alone with her thoughts.

xxx

Curtis was getting ready to head home when Lizzie walked in.

"Made it," she announced.

"That must have been quite a walk." Curtis smiled. "You sound better than you did when we talked. I hope the fresh air helped to clear out those negative thoughts."

"Kinda."

"I can't say I know what you're going through, but I do know that having family is very important. And if you don't feel connected to anyone, that's a very lonely feeling."

"It is."

"So, I get why this is important to you.

Don't second guess yourself. The trick is to follow your path, but do so slowly, with a lot of caution. Try not to have unrealistic expectations. Just be prepared for whatever may come."

"And what do you think the 'whatever may come' is?"

"I don't know. But you should be prepared to hear that your mother doesn't want anything to do with you. It's a real possibility. But don't let it discourage you. You sounded so bummed out on the phone. Remember, if you never try to find what you're looking for, how will you ever know if the journey is worth it?"

"What the hell does that mean?"

Curtis laughed. "It just means don't give up at the first rough turn. You don't strike me as the type to give up. Or to cave to what anyone asks of you."

Lizzie thought that sounded like something Eileen would say. How Lizzie was strong and could make her own life. But then she thought about the night with Deena and the fat man in the suit. *How wrong Curtis is about me*, she thought. *Was Eileen wrong too?* "I'm not always brave," Lizzie said. "Sometimes I go along because it's easier."

"You? A pushover? We're going to have to fix that if you're going to survive here in Kingston! Let's go."

Lizzie followed Curtis to his car. She had a lot to think about on the short drive to Curtis's house.

As they pulled into the driveway, Lizzie looked around. The lawn was perfectly laid out with sunflowers and trimmed hedges and a wooden gate led to the front of the house. The modest blue home looked welcoming.

Curtis's wife, Gail, was standing in the living room waiting to greet them when they arrived. Lizzie was struck by how pretty she was. Her thick blonde hair was pulled back into a ponytail. Her big green eyes were highlighted by carefully applied makeup.

Lizzie was surprised Curtis was married to a white woman. Curtis was always talking about racial equality and the empowerment of his people, like Cassie. Lizzie thought of Stella back at Chelsea, and how she hated white people because she felt they got away with everything. And how Cassie said the white girls in the complex got away with things girls of colour could not. With Curtis's talk about preserving black culture, Lizzie thought Curtis would see white people as a threat, too. Looking at Gail, Lizzie decided she must have been wrong about Curtis. About what it meant to be black. Clearly, not all black people felt the same or thought the same.

The more Lizzie learned about what it meant to be a person of colour, the more she realized how little she knew. And how much more she needed to learn.

Chapter 15

Surprise

"You must be Lizzie. I'm so happy to meet you." Gail smiled.

"Same here," said Lizzie shyly. "Thank you for inviting me."

"Speaking of which, I have a nice dinner keeping warm in the kitchen. I hope you like Cornish hen."

"I do." Lizzie followed Curtis and Gail to the dining room. Soon Gail had the table covered with a complete meal. Small stuffed chickens and everything to go with them, from mashed potatoes to beans and pasta salad. Lizzie hadn't seen a spread that great since Priya's parents' anniversary potluck.

"You didn't have to do all this for me." Lizzie tried to be modest. But she was thrilled by the idea of eating her first full home-cooked meal since she had left Joshua Creek.

"It was no trouble," said Gail, laughing. She must have seen the hunger in Lizzie's eyes. "Those tiny hens take no time at all to prepare. When Curtis called me this morning, I didn't want to just make hotdogs."

Curtis chuckled. "As if you ever make hotdogs."

Gail nudged him with her elbow and grinned.

Lizzie could tell there was a solid bond between this couple. They gave off a good energy. She thought about Damon. It wasn't like that with him. She wished she'd had that with Damon. If she did, maybe he would have wanted their baby. Maybe he would be in Kingston with her now, helping to find her mother.

"Sit, Lizzie," Curtis said.

As they all sat down and dove into the food, Gail wasted no time bombarding Lizzie with questions.

"So, Lizzie, forgive me if I seem a bit nosy. Don't feel like you have to answer, if you're not comfortable with my questions."

"It's okay."

"Curtis said you were just seventeen. Can I ask what your adoptive parents felt about you coming to Kingston to look for your birth mother?"

Lizzie was ready to share the tensions she'd been having with Eileen. It was good to talk to someone other than Priya about it. "My mother is totally against this."

"Really?" Curtis looked surprised.

"We don't really get along," said Lizzie.

"And why is that?" Gail swallowed a bite of food.

"I've never been exactly sure. But I think we're just very different."

"Mother-daughter stuff?"

"It's a little more complicated than that. I grew up in Joshua Creek. My parents are white, and so are all their friends. Not that all my parents' friends were racist, but they definitely had their noses way up in the air. They didn't understand why my parents were raising a black baby in their neighbourhood or bringing her to their social events. They were sure I would turn out to be trouble. You know, fail in school, or get into drugs or something."

"Lizzie, that is racist!" Curtis said.

"Yeah, but I think in their way my parents stood up for me."

"Well, at least there's that."

Sensing Curtis's sarcasm, Lizzie felt like she had to come to her parents' defence.

"I remember one time my parents took me to an awards ceremony where my dad was the guest of honour. I was about eight. He'd bought me a blue and gold silk dress for the occasion. I felt like a princess. But not everyone there saw me that way. I was the only black kid in the room. Not just the only black kid, but the only black person. I knew I was different. My dad took me to use the bathroom, and I overheard his boss talking to him outside the door. He asked my father how he could do it."

"Do what?" Gail asked.

"Raise a black child."

"What did your father say?" Gail asked.

"He asked if it was only white children who were deserving of love. And he said he couldn't imagine his life without me in it. I heard his boss tell him not to be so defensive before he walked off."

"How sweet," said Curtis pointedly.

Gail shushed him so Lizzie could go on.

"When I came out of the bathroom, my dad knew I'd heard everything. He knelt in front of me and asked if I was hurt. I told him I was. He asked me how he could fix it, and

I said I wanted to kick his boss in the knees. So, he marched me out to where his boss was sitting with his wife and some other people."

"Really?" Now Curtis was intrigued.

"So, we walk up to the table and my dad taps his boss on the shoulder." Lizzie made a tapping gesture. Her arm caught the beans and rice dish and tipped it over.

"Oops, sorry." She was embarrassed.

"No, keep going," Gail ordered as she wiped up the spilled beans.

"My dad's boss turns around and tries to give me a smile. A really phony smile. So, I kicked him as hard as I could."

Gail clapped and squealed happily. "What did he do?"

"Nothing. He yelled out in pain, of course. But he said nothing. He knew why I did it. Then we left. My dad did not want to stay and accept his boss's bullshit award."

"Lizzie, you didn't mention your mother in that story," Curtis prompted.

"On the drive home, she and my dad argued. She told me to listen to music on my phone so I couldn't hear. But I could hear. My mom was pissed. She told my dad what he did just supported the worst stereotypes about black people and violence. All I knew was that she was angry with me for what I had done, when I felt so good about it."

To Lizzie's surprise, Stella popped into her mind. When Stella gave in to her anger and beat up someone — beat up Lizzie — did she feel good? Did she feel like Lizzie did at that moment?

"It sounds like your parents had very different ways of standing up for you, Lizzie," Curtis said. Then he asked gently, "Is that why you want to find your birth mother?"

"Partly, I guess," Lizzie said, coming back to the present. "I always wondered. And it became even more important to me when I got pregnant."

"Pregnant?!" Curtis and Gail both shouted.

Lizzie realized the beans on the table weren't the only ones she had spilled.

Chapter 16

An Uncertain Future

Priya: so give me the dirt, how'd it go at the couple's house?

Lizzie: too much to text. Call me

Priya: long diatnce, you call me

Lizzie: ur so cheap! And you spelled distance wrong!

Priya: call me!!!

Lizzie laughed as she dialed Priya's number.

"Why do you do this to me?" Priya said without a hello. "You know I can't stand it when you have juicy gossip and you don't share."

"Not sure how juicy it is. It was just dinner."

"No, it wasn't. They're going to help you find your birth mother."

"Correction. They're going to try to help."

"What else?"

"Oh, I told you Curtis is black. But I didn't find out until the dinner that his wife is white."

"No way."

"Yup. But oh, Priya, she is so nice." Lizzie could hear Priya's TV playing in the background. "That sounds like our show," Lizzie said wistfully.

Both of them had become obsessed with a show called *Making It Work*. The main characters had travelled together to Hollywood to try to make it as actors. But the journey was tougher than the young people had imagined. They often ended up hustling or working crazy jobs to get by.

"It is," confirmed Priya. "Did you see last week's episode?"

"I've missed the last few. I don't have a TV." Lizzie sighed.

"Why?"

"I don't have enough money."

"Lizzie! What do you mean you don't have enough money? Call your mom and get some. This is crazy."

"You know I can't do that, Priya. What do you want me to say? 'Hey, Mom, I used your credit card for an Airbnb that I never stayed in. I hope they put the refund back on your card. And I got beat up by a big, mean black girl in a homeless shelter. Oh, yeah, and I had a funky three-way with a tall redhead and a fat businessman in a small suit. I used the two hundred dollars I got from that to buy bedsheets, prenatal pills, and groceries. Gosh, how could I forget to mention I'm pregnant. So, can you send money so I can make an even bigger mess of my life?'"

"Lizzie, you are so stubborn!"

"It's not as easy as you think, Priya."

"I can send you a few dollars. I'd have to figure out something to tell my dad, though, because he watches my banking activity."

"No way. I'm not getting you caught up in my mess. Your dad would really hate me."

"Lizzie, that social worker and his wife — you know what this means, right?"

"No, what?"

"A biracial couple?"

"Weren't we just talking about money?"

"I'm just thinking. A black man and a white woman. Lizzie, they could be your parents!"

Lizzie laughed. She missed Priya and her outrageous theories.

"First of all, neither of them looks anything like me, not even a tiny bit. Second, there's no way Gail would have been so easygoing and pleasant if she thought I could be her long-lost kid."

"I guess you're right." Priya sighed. She wanted to claim victory for having solved Lizzie's mystery. "I saw Eileen at the market yesterday. She asked me about you. I didn't even know what to say. Girl, you haven't called your mom since you left? I thought you said you two had been speaking."

"I lied. I've been wanting to call her, Priya. But I don't know how to break it to her that I'm pregnant. And that I've been here for a whole month and am still no closer to finding my birth mother than when I first got here."

"Do you really think she'd care about that? Stop being so stubborn and call her."

"Honestly, what do you think my mom would say about me being pregnant?"

"I think she would tell you not to keep it."

Lizzie thought about it. Maybe Priya was right. Maybe her mom would think Lizzie wasn't ready for a baby. Lizzie often thought the same thing.

"There is absolutely nothing wrong with

admitting you're not ready to raise a child, Lizzie," said Priya. It was like she could read Lizzie's mind. "Adoption is a beautiful thing for a family who really wants a baby. Look at you. You didn't turn out so bad. You had a mother who cared enough to let you go so you could have a better life. And were raised by a mom who gave you the freedom to follow your heart."

"Seriously, how did you get so wise, Priya?"

"Think about it, Lizzie. Everything you know in your life will change once that baby comes. You're out there in Kingston alone, trying to get your shit together. You need to let Eileen help."

Lizzie hated when Priya said things she didn't want to hear. But she knew her best friend was making sense. Would giving her baby to a stable family be the best thing for the child? Would it give her baby the chance to have the stability Eileen and Bill had given Lizzie? Or would she be sentencing her baby to a lifetime of trying to fill the same hole Lizzie felt in her life? The hole that led her to the beating by Stella, and the nightmare sexual encounter with Deena. Lizzie realized she had a lot of thinking to do.

She once wondered how a mother could spend all those months bonding with her baby, just to give it away to someone else. For the last month, she had been feeling the sting of being faced with that very decision. She wondered if her birth mother had felt the same way when she was pregnant with Lizzie. If her birth mother had thought those same uncertain thoughts. Lizzie questioned the strength of the bond with her baby. She wondered if love and the desire to do the right thing could cause her to follow in her birth mother's footsteps. Lizzie realized she no longer had just herself to think about. Every decision she made would change her baby's future forever.

Chapter 17

Hope

Lizzie rubbed her hands across her belly. Her pregnancy was still not showing, even though she was nearing her twelfth week. She had never thought about her thin frame, but she felt like the growth of her stomach should be hugely obvious by now. She had started attending the mandatory Friday evening parenting sessions in the big classroom downstairs. She had plenty of questions for their facilitator, Rita. Some of the girls were much farther along in their pregnancies than Lizzie was, and she hadn't been attending the group very long. But she felt the last few sessions had taught her a lot about everything that went into caring for a baby. Especially all the sacrifices parents make as their baby grows up.

Hearing Rita talk about parenting gave Lizzie a newfound appreciation for the work her own parents had put into raising her. They didn't have to take in Lizzie. Instead, they made the choice that they wanted to love and care for her. Lizzie had never thought about it as much as she had in the last few weeks. But the more Lizzie learned, the more difficult her choices were becoming. She had to start thinking seriously about whether she was ready to take on the big commitment of keeping her baby. It wouldn't be a job for a few months or a year. It would be a commitment for the next eighteen years. Lizzie couldn't even imagine where she would be in two months, not to mention two years, or eighteen.

Lizzie picked up her phone and saw she

had missed several texts from Curtis. She called him back.

"Hey, Lizzie, sorry to blow your phone up. I just wanted to pass on some news that may be helpful to you."

"Okay," said Lizzie. She didn't know whether to be excited or not.

"Gail spoke to one of the older nurses at the hospital. Her name is Cora Lee? Cora Anne? Something like that. Anyway, she's been a nurse for about thirty years, ready to retire soon, I think. Gail sat with her at lunch today and talked about her work in the maternity ward the year you were born."

Lizzie was intrigued. "And what did she have to say?"

"A lot of stuff. Most importantly, she remembered the women who didn't plan to keep their babies. You see, around that time, Ontario legalized same-sex marriage."

"So? What does that have to do with me? Wait! Was my mother a lesbian?"

"No. I mean, I have no idea, Lizzie. That's not where I was going with this."

"Okay, talk faster then."

"The nurse remembered those years because they had a whack of same-sex couples wanting to adopt babies. Married couples stood a better chance of adopting than people who were seen as single."

"Even if you were gay and with a partner?"

"Well, that was also a huge hurdle. But that's a story for another day. Gail asked Cora about biracial babies. She said she remembered three in particular. She says there were three mothers with mixed-raced babies who were not planning to keep them."

"So, they just gave babies away at the hospital like that?"

"No, of course not. There was an adoption social worker who worked with the hospital. They sometimes arranged to have meetings at the hospital and sometimes the couples would go to see specific babies in the ward. There was much fuss and paperwork that had to happen. But couples wanted to eye the babies in the ward like they were shopping for teacups in a china shop. At least that's what Cora says."

"So, I could have been adopted by a same-sex couple?"

"That was a possibility, sure."

"But I wasn't. Did the nurse remember any of the names?"

"Of the same-sex couples?" Curtis joked.

"No, Curtis, the mothers."

He laughed. "There's one thing she did remember from the month you were born. All the women who had mixed-race babies were white women. Which means your mother was white, and your father would have been black. Gail told Cora the last name you had, Collins. Sure enough, Cora remembered there being a Collins on the ward. She remembered her because she used to tease the woman about being a diva like Joan Collins. Isn't that crazy? You can't make this stuff up."

"Who's Joan Collins?"

"Only one of the biggest evening soap stars on TV that ever lived."

"Soap star?"

"Gosh, you are so young. *Dynasty* was the name of a popular show. Even I know that. One of the characters was a villain named Alexis Carrington, the most popular woman on the show. She was played by an actress named Joan Collins."

"So, Cora only remembered this mother because her last name was the same as some villain on TV?" Lizzie wasn't sure what it all meant for her. She was excited and afraid at the same time.

"Cora wants to meet you, Lizzie. I think you should do it. Gail and I can be right there with you if you want. Maybe this woman is not your birth mother, but maybe she is. At the very least, Cora could answer some of your questions. And meeting with you might jog her memory and help her remember some other things."

"Can I think about it first?" Lizzie didn't know why, but she was scared.

"Of course."

After Lizzie said goodbye to Curtis, she tried hard to not think about what he had revealed. At least for a while. But she was confused about what to do. All she had wanted was to meet her real mother. And now the chance seemed to be close. But the nagging thoughts of whether to raise her baby alone or let it go were overshadowing any happiness or excitement she should be feeling. And her mind dwelled on her doubts about whether her birth mother would even want to meet her. And about what kind of life she and her family — if she had a family — were living. She decided she would get through her parenting session first, then call Curtis back about meeting with Cora.

Chapter 18

Feeling Squeamish

Rita was setting up her laptop and projector when Lizzie walked in.

"Hey, Rita!" she said.

"Oh, hi, Lizzie."

"Are we watching a movie or something?"

"Sort of. At the end of the session, we're going to watch a video of a baby being delivered."

Lizzie squished up her face.

Rita laughed. "That will be you in just a few

months, Lizzie. So, it's better to see it now for the first time than when you're on the delivery table."

Lizzie thought about that. A few months was not a lot of time. She didn't feel ready.

"Would you mind grabbing those, Lizzie?" Rita asked, pointing at a stack of pamphlets. "Just put them on the table."

There were a few girls who always strolled into the class late. Lizzie made sure to put out extra pamphlets for them. She felt that casually walking in late was disrespectful of Rita's time. Eileen had taught Lizzie to always be on time, or even early. So, Lizzie usually arrived about ten minutes before the session started, and ended up helping Rita prepare. Lizzie didn't mind helping. In fact, she enjoyed getting to know Rita. The time alone with her also gave her the chance to ask the questions she was too ashamed to ask in front of the others. She felt shy asking why her breasts were so sore, or why the very smell of (or even the thought of) garlic or eggs made her vomit.

Rita took Lizzie's questions in stride and answered her directly. Rita reminded Lizzie of her favourite English teacher. They were both very smart and entertaining, even in front of a room full of rude teenagers. Lizzie had thought the two women even looked alike. But now, when she looked closer, at Rita's straight dark hair, designer eyeglasses, and her fashionable style, she realized she wasn't like her teacher at all. Lizzie wondered if she was making more of their similarities than what was there. Maybe she was just missing school life, which seemed a world away from her now.

Before she'd met Damon, Lizzie had thought about how she would go to university and study English. Now that felt like a wishful dream. It made Lizzie sad to think about no longer having the encouragement of her teacher. Lizzie also knew it must have saddened her mom that she wasn't in school. And certainly, her dad would have been disappointed in her. Lizzie decided it was probably Rita's attentiveness that reminded her of the English teacher, and not so much her looks.

"How have you been feeling, Lizzie?" Rita's voice broke into her thoughts. "Still a lot of morning sickness?"

"Yes," she mumbled as she handed Rita the rest of the pamphlets.

"Don't worry. It usually subsides after the first trimester."

"I sure hope so. I can't wait to eat a normal plate of food again. I'm gonna pile it as high as I can, then eat like a pig in its pen!"

"I experienced morning sickness and childbirth once. It was no fun."

Lizzie hadn't realized Rita was a mother. But it made sense. Rita was a good instructor for the sessions, answering all their questions like she knew what she was talking about. "You have a kid, Rita?"

"I didn't say I had a kid. I said I went

through morning sickness and gave birth before." Rita's look changed from pleasant to offended.

"Oh." Lizzie could tell her prying wasn't welcome. Maybe Rita's baby had died. Lizzie tried to change the subject before it became uncomfortable for both of them. "Why does it happen, though? I mean, why do you think we get morning sickness?"

"I'm simplifying it a bit, but your body sees your baby as a foreign object. And your body's job is to reject anything that isn't supposed to be there."

"Really?"

"Absolutely. That queasy feeling, sickness, nausea. It all means your body is doing what it's supposed to be doing. Eventually your brain and body catch on that your foreign object isn't going anywhere. Then your body becomes a protector of the baby growing inside."

"That's so amazing."

"It really is. That's why every single baby is

an absolute miracle. When you think of all the intricate things the body goes through just to bring a life into the world . . ."

"Yeah." *Miracle* was exactly the right word.

Lizzie took a seat at the end of the long table as the other girls began walking in. She wasn't keen on having a front row seat to watch a woman's insides on display as her baby came popping out.

When Lizzie spotted Deena walking in, she twisted in her chair. She had been avoiding Deena since that night at her apartment. She'd been ignoring her calls and had left her texts unanswered. Deena hadn't been at the last two sessions, and the rumour was that she was on bedrest. Lizzie doubted that was true. She had figured Deena would be a no-show again, so she was surprised to see her there.

Deena looked at Lizzie and rolled her eyes. For the rest of the evening, she avoided looking in Lizzie's direction, as if that eye contact had said all she wanted to say. It didn't bother

Lizzie. She hoped Deena's eye rolling was a sign she was done with Lizzie. Lizzie had been done with Deena a long time ago.

When the session was over, Lizzie dashed out. She didn't want to get stuck having no choice but to speak to Deena. Lizzie did have more questions for Rita, but she decided to wait until the next session to ask them. As she headed down the hallway, Cassie poked her head out the classroom door and called her back. "Aren't you staying for snacks, Lizzie?" she asked.

"I'm too tired," Lizzie lied.

"Yeah, right. I'll save you a plate." Cassie grinned.

Lizzie waved her off and disappeared. Pita with hummus and raw veggies and dip were her favourite pregnancy snacks. Even after watching the woman on the screen give birth, Lizzie still would have eaten them all. It was just too weird being in the same room with Deena. As much as Lizzie thought she was over the whole incident, seeing Deena brought it all back. Maybe she wasn't as past it as she thought she was.

When Lizzie got to her room, she checked her texts. Nothing more from Curtis. She realized she actually was tired, so she decided to go to sleep.

Chapter 19

Called Home

Early Wednesday morning, Lizzie was awakened by the buzzing of her phone.

It was a text from Priya: u up yet?

Lizzie: yea

Priya: I'm calling you.

Lizzie: Kk

Lizzie answered on the first ring. "I have so much to tell you, Priya. The last few days have been crazy."

"Did you find her?"

"No, but so close. Curtis's wife, Gail, spoke to one of the nurses who was working in the hospital where I was born. She remembered my mother because of her last name, Collins."

"Really?"

"And something about gay people trying to adopt babies from the hospital."

"Huh?" Priya laughed.

Lizzie laughed too, knowing she had that story totally wrong. "Well, I only really heard the part about the nurse remembering my mother. The rest of it was all gibberish."

"Lizzie —"

Lizzie was so excited she cut her friend off. "I've decided I'm going to see this nurse. Curtis and Gail set it all up. They're picking me up Monday and taking me to this woman's house. I can't believe it. I feel like I'm so close."

"Lizzie —"

"We would have done the meeting right away, but I waited a few days before agreeing. And this nurse works three days on and three days off. So, we have to wait until Monday."

"Lizzie —"

"What, Priya? Aren't you excited for me?"

"Lizzie, your mom is very sick."

"What do you mean sick?"

"I mean you have to come home."

"Did she tell you to call me?"

"Yes."

"I knew it. She's trying to make me come back."

"I don't think so, Lizzie. She wanted me to tell you because you haven't contacted her or returned any of her calls."

"Because I'm not ready. I don't have proof that leaving was the right thing to do. Eileen always told me, if I left, she wouldn't be there to support me. Now I'm supposed to go running back to support her?"

"She's your mom, Lizzie. I can't even imagine not dropping everything to be with my mom if she needed me."

"That's a cultural thing, Priya."

"It's also a respect thing, Lizzie."

Lizzie knew Priya was right. There was no way she could leave her mom alone when she was sick. Eileen didn't have any other family.

After Lizzie hung up with Priya, she called her mom.

"Lizzie?" Eileen sounded weak and tired.

"Hi, Mom."

"Lizzie, I'm so happy to hear your voice. It's been so long. I've missed you so much."

"I've missed you too."

"How have you been? Tell me everything that's been happening with you."

Lizzie tried to keep the conversation away from anything that would lead to her mom pressuring her to go home. That would just start an argument. And Lizzie didn't want this phone conversation to end the way her last day at home with her mom had.

"Priya says you're sick," Lizzie said.

"I am."

"What's wrong with you?"

"They think I have stomach cancer."

"Oh no."

"Things have become so unbearable. I can't eat. And I've just been sick all the time."

"I'm so sorry, Mom."

"I have to get an endoscopy done on Monday to see if it really is stomach cancer."

"I hope it's not."

"I told Priya to call you because I need you home. I don't want to go through this alone."

The words sounded selfish to Lizzie's ears. Her mom was trying to make her feel guilty. But Lizzie knew that was just a childish reaction. Suddenly, she felt bad for thinking such harsh thoughts when her mother was clearly not well.

"Will you come, Lizzie?" her mom pleaded. "I'll pay for you to get home."

Lizzie thought about everything she would have to drop to go back to her mother. Her apartment, the friends she'd met, her parenting classes. The meeting with Cora that might lead her to her birth mother. But then Lizzie remembered how her mom had always been there for her when she was not well. Lizzie thought about the baby she was carrying, and wanted her child to have that too. Would Lizzie need her child to be there for her someday, just like Eileen needed Lizzie now? In her head, Lizzie weighed what she had against what she wanted for her child. It made her choice very clear.

"Okay, I'll come."

xxx

The conversation with Curtis and Gail was tough for Lizzie. The three of them met at a cafe on Curtis's lunch break.

"So, what's this news, Lizzie?" Curtis asked. "You had me concerned when you called."

"I won't be able to meet with the nurse on Monday," said Lizzie.

"What?" Gail was shocked. "I put so much into making that happen. It took me a long time to get Cora Lee to open up to me."

"I'm so sorry, Gail," Lizzie apologized. "I don't really have a choice. I was talking to my mom last night. She's really sick. They think she might have cancer."

"Oh no. I'm sorry, Lizzie. I was being selfish." Gail grabbed Lizzie's hand.

"No, you weren't," Lizzie replied. "I know how much you did to try to help me. I feel bad for leaving like this."

"When do you go?" asked Curtis. "Can you at least wait until Tuesday, after you've met with Cora?"

"I can't, Curtis. My mom said she is getting an endo-something done Monday and she wants me there with her."

Curtis frowned.

They all sat and looked at their plates. It was clear no one had much of an appetite. Curtis and Gail fiddled with their lunches. The sight of the sandwich sitting on Lizzie's plate made her feel nauseated.

"I get it," Curtis finally said. "Your mom needs you, and you absolutely should be there with her."

"I'm going to help her get through this." Lizzie nodded. "But I plan to come back to Kingston. I'm not giving up hope of finding my birth mother."

"Cora Lee isn't going anywhere," said Gail. "You do what you need to do, Lizzie. I'll talk to her tomorrow at work and let her know you're leaving. This may be a sign that now just wasn't the time for you and your birth mother to meet."

Lizzie decided Gail might be right. She thought about the challenges she'd faced getting to Kingston and about struggling through her emotional issues. It had been hard. And they might have been signs that the timing just wasn't right. She stood up, hugged Curtis and Gail, and said goodbye. Lizzie had decided that the day after her next parenting session, she would pack up her meagre belongings and head back home.

Chapter 20

Rita

Lizzie was sure that her next parenting session would be her last. She arrived early as usual to take advantage of the time alone with Rita. She had come to really like and respect Rita and felt she should let her know why she wouldn't be coming to any more sessions.

"I'm so sorry to hear you're leaving, Lizzie," said Rita when she heard Lizzie's news. "But I commend you for going to be with your mom. Most of us only get one mother, so we have to take care of them when they need us."

"I guess so," Lizzie said.

"You don't sound excited about going back."

"I have mixed emotions. I know going back is the right thing. But I can't help feeling like I failed."

"What do you mean?"

"Like I'm letting down everyone by not finding the answers I was looking for. I wanted time to find my birth mother so I'd have answers for my own baby. And I wanted to show my mom I could do this."

"I understand."

"Rita, can I ask you a question? I don't want to make you mad."

"Sure."

"Why did you get upset after mentioning you went through childbirth? Did your baby die?"

Rita was silent for a moment. Lizzie could see her searching to find the words to explain.

"I did go through childbirth," Rita finally said. "I was young like you. I was in love with a boy named George. I would have done anything for him. That included sneaking out to go to a dance with him. My parents were very religious and very strict. My sister and I weren't allowed to have boyfriends. Especially not black boyfriends. And I really loved George." Rita sat down beside Lizzie. "But he betrayed me."

"How?"

"After the dance, he took me to his house. He raped me. It was the most painful thing ever. A few weeks later, I missed my period. So, I had to tell my parents I'd had sex."

"Rape isn't sex, Rita."

"I know that now. But I was sixteen. To me it was the same. I had disobeyed their wishes by sneaking out to see George. And that led to me being pregnant."

"How did they react?"

"My father was furious. He refused to speak

to me. My mother sent me to my aunt's house until the baby was born. They didn't believe in abortion. But they let me know right away I wouldn't be allowed to keep the baby. They would be reminded of what a bad daughter I was every time they looked at the child, they said. I would have to relive their judgment, and my pain and shame, every day. And they simply wouldn't let me bring a mixed-race baby home. You have no idea how hard it was to carry a new life, knowing I would never be able to name or love my baby, or watch my child grow up."

"Rita, that's so sad. Did you at least get to see it?"

"Him. It was a boy. That's all I knew. And that's only because the doctor announced it when he came sliding out of me. I'll never forget the sound of his cry."

Rita's words made Lizzie want to cry. "Do you ever wonder what he looks like, Rita? Or what it would have been like to raise him on your own?"

"I was never in a position to raise a baby on my own. I was still a child myself when he was born. Having a baby should be something planned between two people. Parents should love each other and commit to raising their child in a loving environment. On purpose. I didn't have that. And George made me swear the baby wasn't his, even though it was. I don't know how I would have felt about him . . . the baby, knowing what his father did to me, how he came into the world."

Lizzie started thinking about her own situation. Damon had claimed to love her, then left her as soon as she got pregnant. It wasn't the brutal situation Rita described, but still, Lizzie knew how it felt to be alone. Rita had known she couldn't care for her baby. Lizzie wondered if she was being selfish wanting to raise her baby alone, without the support of the father. Without the support of Eileen.

"Lizzie, I share this with you because I've really grown to care about you and your situation. If my experience can help with your decision about what to do, I'm happy some good might come of it. I do wonder about my baby. But it's been so long. I would never try to find him or disrupt his life."

"I wonder if my birth mother feels the same way."

"She probably has, many times. It's not an easy choice to give a baby up for adoption. I never had a choice. Maybe your mother did. Maybe she wanted you to have a life better than what she could give you. That's why you need to think very carefully what to do if you do find your birth mother. It would be hard for both of you if you just showed up in her life out of the blue. There are too many unknowns. Wherever my son is, I hope he is safe and happy. But for both of us, it was better to just let it be."

Rita got up to get a tissue to wipe away some stray tears. Lizzie felt bad that she had made her open up about such a sad story, but she was honoured that Rita had shared her experience. Rita's last words echoed in Lizzie's head. Rita had made peace with her decision. It was clear Rita thought that if her son appeared "out of the blue," it would bring nothing but pain to the both of them. Lizzie imagined growing up being a symbol of such pain and anger. She compared that to her own life, treasured by Bill and Eileen. She agreed Rita was wise to "just let it be."

As Rita collected herself and got ready for the session, Lizzie watched her, thinking about how brave she was. No one would suspect what Rita had been through. Maybe Rita's passion for teaching the classes was her way of helping other young pregnant girls. A way to honour the baby she had given up so she could have a better life.

Chapter 21
The Return

Lizzie's Uber ride home was long and expensive. Eileen had put the ride on her credit card, and she was sure to let Lizzie know how much she had to pay for it during one of their phone calls. How much she had to pay . . . *for my mistakes*, Lizzie felt like adding to the end of her mom's sentence. But she smiled and wondered if the Airbnb charges had been refunded to the card.

When Lizzie arrived home, she walked in the door, dropped her bags, and ran to where her mom was lying on the sofa.

"Welcome back." Lizzie's mom smiled. She looked worn out.

Lizzie stroked her hair. "How are you feeling?"

"I'm good, Lizzie. Even better now that you're here."

"Can I get you anything?"

"No, no. I can barely keep anything down."

Me too, Lizzie thought. But now was not the time to tell her mother she was pregnant. That news would have to wait. "What time is your appointment?" she asked.

"Eight-thirty Monday. We'll relax together for the weekend. Catch up. Then we'll go for the appointment. I'm so glad you'll be there with me."

Lizzie thought about her own cancelled Monday meeting with Cora. What would she have found out? Would that meeting have provided the answer to Lizzie's prayers, to finally know who she and her baby belonged to?

"Lizzie, you should go unpack," said her mom. "Then I want to hear all about what happened in Kingston."

Lizzie grabbed her bags and went up to her room. It was exactly as she'd left it. The bed was perfect, as if someone had freshly made it up that day. The curtains were wide open, showing the stillness of the large homes across the street. She wondered if her mom had even entered the room while she was gone. In the movies, when a mother really missed her kid, she would go into their room and sit on the bed and cry. She had a hard time imagining her mom doing that.

After Lizzie had put her things away, she went back downstairs. She knew her mother would want to know every detail about her time in Kingston. She tried to decide what she would tell her, and what she just wasn't ready to share.

"Come and sit, Lizzie." Her mom sat up and swung her legs onto the floor. As Lizzie plopped down beside her, she said, "This means a lot to me, having you here."

"I know. You've said it already."

"But I don't think you understand. It's been a very scary time for me. Since your dad died, I haven't had anyone to lean on but you. And then you were gone too. I think I fell into a dark depression. I couldn't find my way out."

"What about all your friends? Why weren't they here to give you support?"

"Marla and Allison have been great. But really, my friends are busy with their own lives. And it's not the same as family, you know."

"I know. But I was so close to finding my birth mother. I'm not saying that to make you feel bad. It's just that the timing of you being sick ended that chance."

"I didn't plan to get ill, Lizzie."

"I know. I know. It just wasn't meant to be, I guess."

"I need family right now. Otherwise there's nothing else to fight for."

"Okay."

"Look, I know finding your birth family is important to you. I couldn't get my head around it before. I realize I was trying to stop you, not for you, but for myself. I kept picturing you finding your birth mother and having this amazing relationship. One that you and I never had. And I couldn't bear the pain of that."

"It's not a competition, Mom."

"I know. I'm just telling you how I felt."

"If you were so concerned about our relationship, why was it the way it was? You never did much to make it better."

"I tried. I don't think you ever really understood what I was doing."

"I think that goes both ways."

Lizzie could see her mom was unsure how to respond.

Eileen smiled and brushed Lizzie's scattered curls from her face. "You were the most beautiful baby we'd ever seen, your dad

and I. Just perfect, with those big brown eyes.
I always thought you and I would be so close.
I couldn't wait for you to get older so we could
do girl things together."

"I always thought you resented my skin
and my kinky hair and my culture."

"Is that how you feel?"

"That's how you made me feel."

"That was never my intention."

"But it's how I felt."

"I'm sorry, Lizzie. Being here alone and
sick, I've had so much time to think about
things. I know where I went wrong with you.
I never helped you understand why I was so
demanding. I wanted the very best for you, to
overcome all those stupid stereotypes. But I'm
afraid it came across to you as my not caring.
My not loving you for the wonderful person
you are and that you can be. You and me not
being close is my fault. But I want us to figure
out how we can make it better."

Lizzie's phone buzzed as a text came in.

Priya: r u back?

Lizzie: yea

Priya: what's it like?

Lizzie: strange

Priya: what r u up to?

Lizzie: talking with Mom

Priya: wanna go to Dave's for ice cream then?

Lizzie: you buying?

Priya: LOL! yeah I'll buy

"Mom, I'll be right back, okay? Priya wants to go for ice cream."

"Really, Lizzie? We're in the middle of something."

"We'll talk when I get back."

"Will we? I mean, you just got here and you're leaving already."

Lizzie needed to get away from her mom for a while. She thought going to meet Priya was the right thing to do, even though her mother would feel she was being selfish for leaving. It wasn't about the ice cream. It was about trying to do things differently. Her mom was trying to give them a new start. And Lizzie wasn't the same girl who had left Joshua Creek. She felt that understanding everything — her mom, her birth mother, race and expectations — was possible. But it still felt just beyond her reach.

"Just go back to resting, Mom. We'll finish talking when I get back."

xxx

"Hi, Mrs. Randall," Priya called out from the front door when Lizzie opened it.

"Bring her right back, Priya."

Lizzie rolled her eyes. But she went back to give her surprised mom a quick hug before she headed out the door.

Chapter 22

A Different Girl

Lizzie and Priya walked to Dave's together, happy to be back in each other's company. When they got to the ice cream shop, most of the usual weekend crowd was there. It was a warm spring day, and kids were hanging outside and in the older boys' cars, trying to stay cool with sundaes and cones. Most of them spoke to Lizzie, some to just say hello, others looking for the scoop on where she'd been and why she was back. She tried to dodge the questions and told them she just had a few things she had needed to take care of. Let them think she was checking out universities or whatever.

As soon as Lizzie and Priya sat down in a booth, Scotty plopped down beside Priya.

"Hey, Scotty." Priya grinned at Lizzie. She knew Lizzie saw Scotty as an uninvited intruder. And he was unwelcomed because of the enormous crush he had on Lizzie.

"Hey, beautiful," he sang across the table to Lizzie.

"Hi, Scotty," she mumbled.

"Can I buy you two fine ladies some sundaes?"

"Yes, please." Priya spoke up before Lizzie had a chance to say no.

Lizzie thought it was cheap and cheesy of Scotty to offer to buy two-dollar sundaes.

When he left to make the purchases, Priya gave Lizzie a look. "Gosh, Lizzie, you are horrible at hiding your feelings. At least smile at the guy. I feel bad for him. He really likes you."

"Priya, even if I did like Scotty back — and I don't — I'm pregnant. So why would I be looking to hook up with anyone?"

"Aww, he'd make a cute dad. Damon doesn't want to."

Lizzie was stunned by Priya's attitude. Priya knew how devastated Lizzie had been by Damon's rejection. How could Priya make light of it?

Priya didn't seem to notice Lizzie's shock. "Scotty might be just the medicine you need to get your mind off all the crazy drama you've got going on."

"Crazy drama? Is that what you call my life?"

"Yeah. You can't tell me you don't realize your life is super complicated."

"Well, it's going to get even more complicated once my baby comes."

"I know, I know," Priya said awkwardly.

Then she smiled and said, "Guess what? I heard back from two universities so far. Full scholarship offers from both! Isn't that wild? Mom and Dad were over the moon."

"That's great, Priya," Lizzie said, accepting the change in subject. "I'm not surprised. You're so smart."

Lizzie was happy for her best friend. At the same time, Lizzie felt bad for the time she'd wasted away from school. There was a time when she had loved it as much as Priya did. Now she was a knocked-up black girl, a high-school dropout, a statistic. It was not how she had ever seen her life going.

Scotty returned with the sundaes, including one for himself. He made himself comfortable in the booth. "How was your trip, Lizzie?" he asked. "Weren't you gone to find your birth family?"

"That's a nosy question, Scotty," Lizzie snapped. "And I thought you couldn't eat dairy."

"I take a pill now. So, how's that nosy? Priya told me all about it."

"I didn't mean for you to get all up in Lizzie's business," Priya grumbled.

"I didn't find them," Lizzie replied, tired of the banter.

"That's a bummer." Ice cream dripped from the corner of Scotty's mouth. He wiped it away with his sleeve.

"I'm fine with it," Lizzie fibbed.

"Maybe one day they'll find you."

"Maybe." How she wished that was true.

"Lizzie," broke in Priya, "did you know Scotty got a scholarship to a school in the States?"

"How would I know that, Priya?"

Priya turned to Scotty. "I think what Lizzie meant to say is 'congratulations.'"

"What's the scholarship for, Scotty?" Lizzie asked.

"I don't want to brag, but you're looking at a baseball pitcher destined for the major leagues." Scotty beamed.

"Okay, well, congratulations, then. I hope you go pro."

"That would only be sweet if you were by my side. I need a hot girl cheering me on in the stands. What are the chances of you coming to the States for school?"

Nonexistent, Lizzie thought.

When they finished their sundaes, Priya said pointedly, "Thanks for the treat, Scotty. Lizzie and I have some catching up to do. Maybe you can catch up with Lizzie later."

"That would be great," said Scotty. "Lizzie, can I get your number?"

"No."

"Ouch." Scotty's smile dimmed for a second.

"Let me talk to her," Priya said. "I may be able to change her mind."

Scotty's smile returned as he gathered the trash from the table. "I'll see you pretty girls later."

Once Scotty was out of earshot, Lizzie turned on her friend. "Priya, why would you lead him on like that?"

"I was just playing around. Why are you so angry?"

"Because you're acting foolish. I don't like Scotty that way, and you know I don't. You're giving him hope for something that's never gonna happen."

"It's just a game, Lizzie. Lighten up."

"That's the problem, Priya. You're still into playing games with boys. I'm pregnant. I don't get to play games anymore. Soon I'm going to be somebody's mother."

"You said you weren't planning to keep the baby."

"I've changed my mind so many times. But I feel like this baby needs me."

"Well, don't get mad because I can still fool around and you can't. It's innocent fun and I'm seventeen. I mean to have fun this summer before I go off to university."

Lizzie felt a pang at the reminder that she wasn't going anywhere. "I guess we just don't have the same interests anymore." She glared at Priya.

"Really, Lizzie?"

"Really."

"Okay."

Priya got up from the booth and stormed out.

Lizzie felt bad for making Priya so angry, but she felt they weren't speaking the same language. Her life was about to completely change with the birth of her baby, and she wanted Priya to be a part of that. But she couldn't allow herself to get caught up in teen girl stuff anymore when her problems were giant-sized adult ones.

As she walked home alone, Lizzie wondered if her impatience with Priya was really about becoming a mother, or if it was more about her resentment of the path that Priya was on. The one they were supposed to follow together: Graduation. Summer vacation touring Europe. First year of university together, then on to their careers. The news of Priya's scholarships affected Lizzie more than she wanted to admit. Lizzie was the one who had dropped the ball on their plans. Priya had every right to be angry.

When Lizzie got home, she found her mom asleep on the sofa. Instead of waking her, Lizzie went to the kitchen and tried to put together a meal she could stomach. She turned the stove up high as she tried to fry a porkchop. Within minutes the smoke alarm went off.

Lizzie's mom rushed into the kitchen. Without saying a word, she leapt into action. She turned off the burner, turned on the stove fan, and opened the windows. Once she had things under control, she started laughing. Lizzie couldn't help herself and started giggling too.

"Sit down." Eileen motioned for Lizzie to sit at the table. "I'll make you something to eat."

Lizzie gladly sat down and watched her mom fry another porkchop.

"I see cooking isn't something you got to master in Kingston," her mom said, lifting her eyebrows.

"Hey, Mom, it was your job to teach me."

"Okay, tomorrow we start by boiling an egg."

Lizzie couldn't believe she and her mom were chuckling and kidding around. It had been a long time since they had been so relaxed with each other. Eileen placed the perfectly fried porkchop on a plate in front of Lizzie and watched as she gobbled it all down, piece by piece. Lizzie was surprised by how great it felt to be looked after, to not have to do everything for herself. It was exactly what she needed after the tiff she'd had with her best friend.

Chapter 23

I Know What I Have

Lizzie played games on her cellphone as her mom slept in the recovery room. Finally, the nurse announced that Eileen was free to go. Her mom's friend Marla arrived to pick them up. Lizzie had always thought Marla disliked her. In the past, Marla had told Lizzie she needed to show Eileen more respect for taking her in and raising her. Lizzie stayed silent the whole drive back.

"Are you coming in, Marla?" Eileen asked

as they pulled into the driveway.

"Sure, I can come in for a bit," replied Marla.

When they got inside, Marla helped Eileen out of her jacket and sat with her on the sofa. When Eileen asked Lizzie if she could make all of them some tea, Marla said, "I'll do that." She jumped up and dashed to the kitchen before anyone had a chance to object.

Lizzie looked across the room at her mom. "Why did I even come back? You have her here."

"Don't be silly, Lizzie. She's just trying to be helpful. Come and sit beside me, darling."

Lizzie snuggled next to her mom. The warmth of her mom's arm around her reminded her of when she was little. Maybe Eileen's illness was a sign of things changing between them. If her mom was beginning to soften, Lizzie figured it was time she did the same. After all, she would soon be someone's mother, just like Eileen.

Eileen kissed Lizzie's forehead. "I wish I had your childhood to do all over again," she said. It was like she was reading Lizzie's mind.

"Me too," Lizzie agreed.

"But we don't get second chances when it comes to the choices we make as parents. All we can do is try to fix it going forward."

"You're right." Lizzie knew she couldn't keep her secret from her mom any longer. "Mom, I have something important to tell you."

Just then, Marla popped back into the living room carrying a tray with three cups of tea.

"Nice and hot!" she sang out.

"Lizzie and I were just talking about motherhood, Marla," said Eileen. "I've made so many mistakes, I wish we could get do overs."

"All we can hope for is that our children take what we taught them and make better choices," Marla said pointedly. "Isn't that right, Lizzie?"

Her tone caused Lizzie's blood to boil. She'd had enough of Marla judging her, like she was never good enough to compare to Marla's perfect children. "As I was saying, Mom, I have something I need to tell you." Lizzie spoke to her mom but was glaring at Marla.

"I guess I should leave you two alone," said Marla. She frowned and shot a warning look at Lizzie. "Eileen, if you need anything, just call me."

"Thank you for all your help, Marla," said Eileen.

Once Marla had left, Eileen looked expectantly at Lizzie. "What's the big news? Did you learn anything more about your birth mother?"

"No, nothing like that," Lizzie said. *I might as well just say it*, she thought. "Mom . . . I'm three months pregnant."

"Lizzie, are you sure?" Eileen choked out.

"One hundred per cent." Lizzie paused. She was ready to explain to her mom why she had really left.

"Lizzie . . ." Eileen wiped away the tea that had spilled from her mouth. "I'm just . . . I mean . . . this is not what I expected to hear when you said you had something to tell me. Is Damon the father?"

"Yes. Are you mad?"

"I'm not sure what I am. Of course, I'm not happy about the timing. You're so young. I wanted so much for you before you had to deal with this." Lizzie could feel all the arguments rushing into her mind. But then her mom took her hand. "Lizzie, what do *you* want?" she asked.

"I'm going to have the baby. I want to keep it."

Eileen wrapped her arms around Lizzie and squeezed her tight.

Lizzie didn't understand what was happening. Where was her mom's outrage? "So, you're not upset?"

"I feel like I should be. I always thought I would be. You know, I never got to hear a

doctor say those words to me; *you're pregnant.*
And so, I'm surprised at what I'm feeling now,
to hear my daughter tell me she's pregnant. All
I can think is that it's a miracle. A baby."

"So, you aren't mad?" She had to ask again
to be sure.

"No, I'm not mad. A baby really is a
miracle. It's the love that brings families closer
together. Believe me, I know. You were our
miracle — your dad's and mine — when you
came along. I can't take that precious feeling
away from you."

Lizzie didn't know what to say.

"Lizzie, I need to be here for you," her mom
went on. "And for your baby. If you've decided
you'll keep your baby, I'll be there every step of
the way. I'll support you through this pregnancy.
I'll help you take care of your child. Don't worry,
Lizzie, we'll do it together, as a family."

Lizzie hugged her mom. She felt like
her heart was melting. Her mom's words
confirmed she was doing the right thing. That

she should keep her baby. That she and the baby would be okay.

Lizzie realized it didn't matter in that moment what Cora had to say, or whether a meeting with her would have led her to her birth mother. Lizzie finally realized what she'd had all along: A mother who had raised her to be whatever she wanted to be. A mother who never let her think that being black meant she was less. Lizzie was safe at home with the mother who had raised her. With that mother's help, she could pass down that kind of family closeness to her own child. And that was everything she needed.

Epilogue

Lizzie and her mom gasped at the same time when Lizzie's cup slipped off the end of the table.

Eileen leapt from her chair. "Got it!" she screeched, grabbing the cup and cradling it between her fingers. Orange juice spilled across her hand.

"Good catch, Mom." Lizzie laughed. Her work covered the table in neat piles. "I'm so clumsy these days."

"Well, juice all over the floor is better than all over your assignments." Eileen chuckled. "Lizzie, I've been watching you since you started that correspondence program. You've been putting in a lot of work. I'm sure you wouldn't want all that effort turned into a sticky mess!"

"Oh, Mom, you have no idea. It's so much work."

"You'll be finished those last few high-school credits in no time. Then you'll be applying to all the best schools. I had a dream that they were all fighting over you."

"Speaking of fighting, how did your boss take the news that you're taking early retirement?"

"Wasn't much she could say. Someone has to be home to look after the baby while you're out learning how to change the world. And speaking of fighting again, I'm glad you and Priya have patched things up."

"Yeah, me too."

Eileen put the juice on the counter and grabbed the oven mitts. She handed them to Lizzie and asked, "Do you want to do the honours?"

Lizzie grinned and took the mitts. "Gotta finish what I started, right?"

Lizzie pulled open the oven and inhaled the delicious smell that filled the room. Her mom smiled as Lizzie gently placed the roasting pan on top of the stove. They beamed at each other.

"I cooked my very first roast chicken," Lizzie squealed with excitement. Just as she had promised, her mom had been teaching Lizzie cooking skills, and Lizzie had found how much she loved making meals.

Eileen clapped with pride. "See what a great student you are, Lizzie?"

Lizzie thought about everything she had learned in the last few months. About race and prejudice. About love and support. About family. She thought about how, without Eileen and Bill's love, she could never be a loving mother to her own baby.

"Thank you, Mom," Lizzie said, tears in her eyes. "For everything."

MARQUIS

Québec, Canada